Jeremy's

Challenge

Dave and Katie's Adventure

Raising a Son

Good reading
James

Kit and Drew Coons

Kit Drew

Challenge Series Book Four
Jeremy's
Challenge
Dave and Katie's Adventure Raising a Son
Kit and Drew Coons

Jeremy's Challenge

ISBN: 978-1-7326256-3-1

Library of Congress Control Number: 2019911877

Illustrations by Julie Sullivan (MerakiLifeDesigns.com)

First Edition

Printed in the United States

23 22 21 20

19 1 2 3 4 5

To all those who decide to be a good man or a good woman whether anyone else does so or not.

Blessed are those who find wisdom,
those who gain understanding.
Proverbs 3:13 (NIV)

Other Books by Kit and Drew Coons

Challenge Series of Novels

Challenge for Two

Challenge Down Under

Challenge in Mobile

Challenge in the Golden State

Science Fiction Novel

The Ambassadors

Life-Skills Books

More Than Ordinary Wisdom

More Than Ordinary Faith

More Than Ordinary Choices

More Than Ordinary Challenges

More Than Ordinary Marriage

More Than Ordinary Abundance

Acknowledgments

This novel would not be possible without professional editing and proofreading by Jayna Richardson. All the artwork is by Julie Sullivan. We also thank our reviewers, Leslie Mercer and Kesler Frost, who read the manuscript and made valuable suggestions.

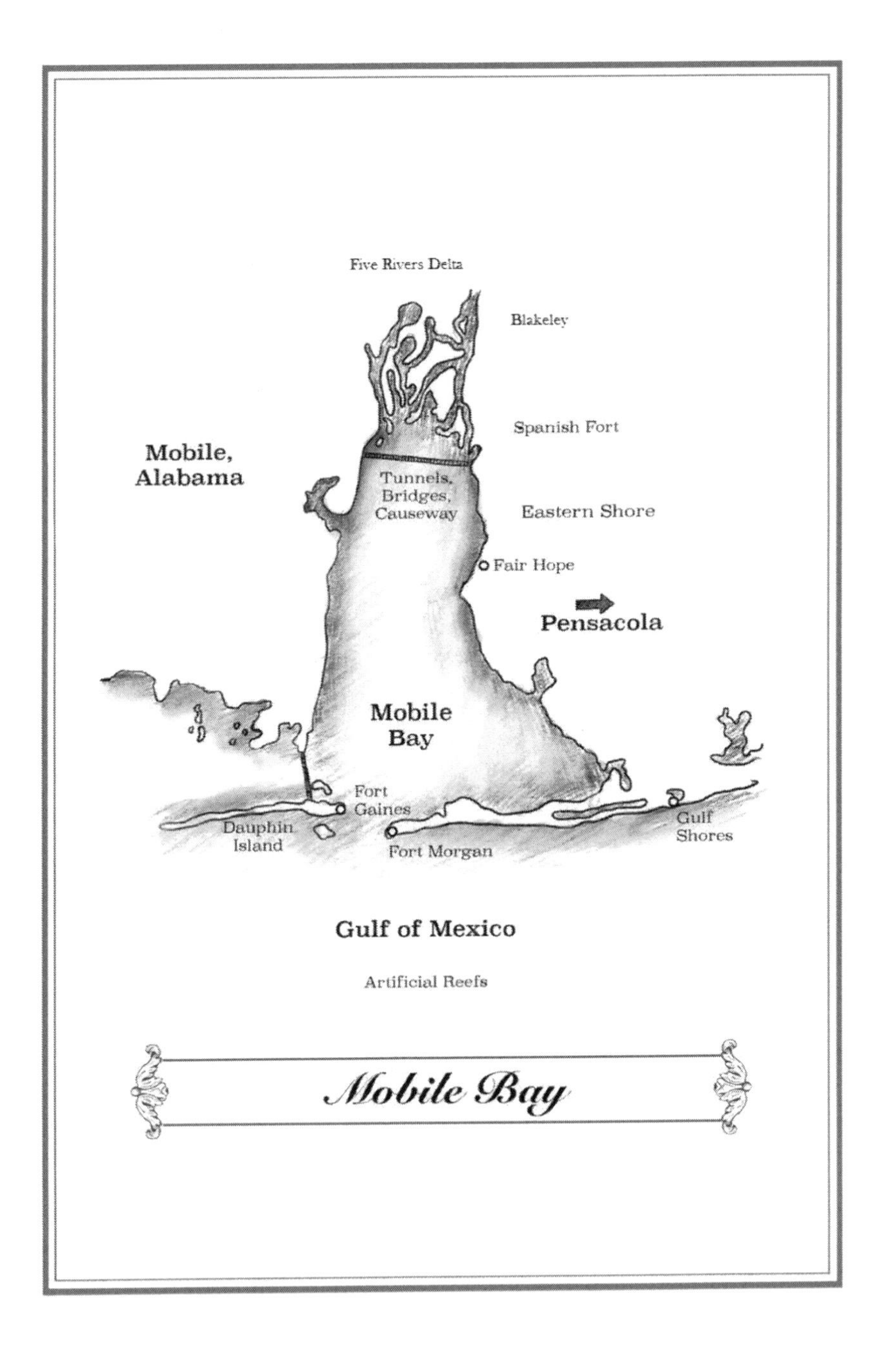
Five Rivers Delta
Blakeley
Spanish Fort
Mobile, Alabama
Tunnels, Bridges, Causeway
Eastern Shore
Fair Hope
Pensacola
Mobile Bay
Fort Gaines
Dauphin Island
Fort Morgan
Gulf Shores
Gulf of Mexico
Artificial Reefs
Mobile Bay

Principal Characters

Jeremy Parker • son of Dave and Katie Parker

Tara Grabowski • a footloose woman

Dave and Katie Parker • Jeremy's parents

Dorothy Goldsmith • secretary/receptionist

Ruthie • Parkers' Labrador retriever

Audit • Parkers' cabin cruiser

Momma (Nancy) Hobbs • a nurturer and lover of children

Poppa (Tom) Hobbs • Momma's husband and restaurant owner

Oliver • Hobbses' teenaged foster son and Jeremy's classmate

Brody Nelson • football prodigy and classmate of Jeremy's

Giselle • member of Jeremy's church youth group

Grandmother McDougall • Katie's mother

Arthur and Sonny • Jeremy's teenaged friends

Officer Vance • Mobile policeman

Daniel Parker • Tennessean, first Parker to Mobile in 1812

Ezekiel Parker • Jeremy's Confederate ancestor

Prologue

* * *

Springtime of my senior year in high school passed without my having made *any* post-graduation plans. If that weren't enough, a major heartbreak had dispirited me about relationships with the fairer sex. Oh, girls interested me almost to a fever pitch. In fear of rejection and humiliation, I admired them from a distance.

My parents couldn't help me relate to the modern culture of 2010. Their old-fashioned values had burdened me for years. Although my heart yearned for travel and adventure, no path leading from my boring existence beckoned. I had no idea what or who I wanted to be.

One immediate concern especially tormented me. Who would I take to the imminent senior prom? In our town, who you took to prom could affect your social status for a lifetime. And after one total heartbreak, I didn't feel like entrusting my future to any of my female classmates. That is, if anyone would even accept my invitation. I had therefore resigned myself to not attending prom.

A less urgent concern was what should I do after graduation. I had not applied to any colleges. No job waited for me. Playing volleyball helped me avoid thinking about my future. I had started playing volleyball at the beach on Dauphin Island because anybody can look cool playing in the sand. Diving headfirst for the ball, whether I got to it or not, always thrilled me. And I wasn't a bad player. Growing nearly a foot during my junior and senior years had made a big difference. And maybe all those years trying to play tennis had given me some measure of coordination. Most important though, I had learned *how* to play by watching the girls' varsity volleyball team. Admittedly, I first attended their matches to watch the girls rather than the sport. Eventually I noticed how the female players emphasized volleyball technique over raw athletic talent, of which I had little.

One Saturday afternoon, as usual, I went to a sports park in the Spring Hill area of west Mobile to play pickup volleyball. But that Saturday I had not yet found a game I could join. An attractive yet bored-looking young woman sat in the early summer sun on a bench nearby. She looked older, certainly already in her twenties. She wore an inexpensive sun hat, athletic top with a bare midriff, and loosely fitting shorts. Shapely tanned legs ended with flip-flops on her feet. Even while sitting, she radiated fitness and self-assurance. A hand-lettered sign at her side offered "Read Your Palm - $5." Something made her different, unlike the girls at school or church. I couldn't take my eyes off her. Looking around to relieve her boredom, she noticed my stare. A surprise to me, being used to demure southern girls, she stared right back, looking directly into my eyes.

Her attention unnerved me. Feeling uncomfortable, I looked away, pretending to watch some pigeons scrapping over a discarded hotdog. After a minute, I risked a glance her way. Her stare remained, except that her face showed a trace of amusement. I quickly diverted my eyes back to the squabbling birds.

As I contemplated a hasty escape, I heard a husky female voice. "Hey, fella. Come over here." When I looked back, she gestured for me to approach. I tried my best to saunter toward her with a mature nonchalance. She gave me an appealing wry smile. "Can I tell you your future?" Her clear, bold voice without any hint of a southern accent sounded exotic to me.

I glanced back at her sign. Five dollars represented a lot of money to me considering the meager allowance Mom and Dad provided. But I heard myself answer, "Sure." My eighteen-year-old voice sounded higher than I had expected, more like a squeak than a confident masculine reply.

"Okay, then sit here next to me." I sat down on her right—a respectable foot and a half away. Her wry smile returned as she removed her sun hat and scooted over until our bare thighs lightly touched. She reached her left hand to take my right wrist and pulled my hand palm-up into her lap. With her right hand she stroked my palm and then up my arm to my elbow. "What's your name?"

I felt my stomach turn over and breath grow shallow. "Jeremy Parker," I managed.

She looked into my eyes from a few inches away. "I'm Tara, Jeremy Parker." Then she leaned over a bit to examine my hand.

My eyes remained on her face as she continued to stroke my arm and study creases in my palm. Tara's features weren't fine like my mother's. But she had a long, appealing face with soft-looking, full lips that hid slightly crooked teeth. Green eyes looked out from under bushy dark eyebrows. Her tanned and slightly flaking skin revealed a lot of time outdoors. A few freckles marked her cheeks. I discerned no makeup. My eyes strayed to her hair: reddish brown knotted into an unkept French braid. Simple stud earrings depicting dolphins pierced her earlobes. I attempted and failed to not look down at her cleavage.

"Well, Jeremy Parker, I see a long life full of adventure and great loves." She glanced up at me. "Do you have a girlfriend?"

I tried to speak more deeply than my previous squeak. "Not officially . . . yet."

Tara investigated my face. The appealing smile returned. "You will have, a guy as cute as you."

I resisted the temptation to lean over and kiss those soft lips. The squeak returned, "You can tell that from my hand?"

"No. I can tell that just by looking at you." Tara tilted her head and frowned slightly. "You like women, don't you?"

"Sure."

"Be a waste, if you didn't." Tara looked back at my palm. "Let's see here. Looks like your parents are old-fashioned. They don't understand you or how things are in 2010."

I couldn't restrain myself from gasping, "That's right!" For the first time I looked at my own palm as if I'd never seen it before.

She traced a crease with her index finger and spoke in a serious tone. "This is your wisdom line. It shows good decision-making ability. You're lucky, Jeremy Parker. Not many fellas your age are so wise. Your wisdom line shows that you crave adventure and new places." She released my hand and sat back. "That's all I can see."

My heart sank when she stopped. Suddenly I became more conscious of our nearness and felt fear. *What would people think if somebody saw me so close to an obviously free-spirited woman?* I scrambled to my feet and fumbled with my wallet. "I owe you five dollars."

"Thank you, Jeremy Parker," she said taking the bill and stuffing it into her shorts pocket. "Do you live nearby?"

"Not far, Mobile." Suddenly, I felt impossibly awkward. "I've got to go."

The wry smile came back. "Okay. See you later, cutie."

At dinner, all I could think of was Tara. I could still feel her holding my hand, stroking my arm. Then I realized Mom had spoken to me over the lasagna. "I asked, did you go to the beach today?" she tried again.

"No, I tried the park."

"What did you do?"

"Just walked around. Looked for a volleyball game."

Mom looked at Dad, who slightly shrugged. They started to discuss something about me. But all I could hear were Tara's words, "See you later, cutie." *Was that her invitation to come back? What a prom date she would make.* I dismissed that thought as too high an aspiration.

* * *

Wait! I'm forgetting that you don't know me. Let me first tell you about the events and circumstances that had brought me to despair before the opportunity of a thousand lifetimes—an opportunity for a true adventure with the beautiful and mysterious Tara—fell into my lap.

Chapter One

* * *

Age fourteen is an awkward time for a young man. You're just old enough to have a house key and watch yourself alone at home. You're much too young to have a car key and take yourself someplace more interesting. Not that Mobile, Alabama, offers much of interest for a teenager. But anyplace at that age is better than being home.

Just as one fledgling bird in the nest gets all the worms, I experienced some advantages from being an only child: my own room, never having to split the last cookie, no hand-me-down clothes to wear. Balance those with two sets of attentive eyes watching my every move—eyes made even more attentive because I had arrived late. A child born after twelve years of my parents struggling to have a baby. Mom and Dad were already old—closer to forty than thirty—before managing just one offspring. At my parents' advanced age, I had precious little chance of a sibling coming to divert any scrutiny from me.

Oaks usually produce thousands of acorns. Each acorn has the potential of producing a mighty tree. After many generations of Parkers and McDougalls, my combined family tree eventually produced just one acorn, me. The only son of two sibling-less parents, the heritage of generations of fishermen and lumbermen rested on me alone. That's a heavy load on a kid.

I probably have distant cousins out there somewhere. But most had dispersed three generations earlier to salary-paying jobs in the big cities. Only a remnant of the hearty pioneers who had scratched out a meager living on the inland waters of the Gulf coast and the depleted forests of Minnesota remained. Both families had dwindled to me, Jeremy, the son of Dave and Katie Parker.

Growing up, Mom had always said to me, "I don't understand why you would do that, Jeremy. That's what bad boys do. But you're a good boy, not a bad boy." Her attempt to instill character, I suppose. But, in truth, I was neither a good nor a bad boy. Just a boy.

Even at an early age, I could tell that my parents retained the values of their forefathers. Traditional would be a kind way to describe them. Kids called people like them "fossils." Mom even used "dinosaur" as a pet name for Dad. Until age seven I had thought that Dad had crawled out of the bayou as a giant lizard and evolved into a man. I later purposed to forge a different path than the traditional rut my fossilized parents had followed.

* * *

Before giving birth to me, my mother had been a science teacher in Mobile's public schools. Once I started school, Mom, with time on her hands, began conducting community science demonstrations for students and sometimes their parents. She could make water freeze in a warm room, create glowing soap bubbles, lay a balloon on a table and have it self-inflate, make a paper clip float on water—things that looked like magic. The kids' favorite was making people talk funny using helium. After each trick, Mom explained the science that caused it to work. The students didn't always understand the science, but she made science cool. This led to Mom pestering Mobile's school board for science resources and getting local businesses to donate supplies. Her efforts evolved into rallying parents to take a part in their kids' schooling.

West of downtown Mobile in the area called mid-town, Mom and Dad owned a large two-story remodeled brick house built in 1926. Live oak trees draped with Spanish moss spread evergreen branches over quiet streets. Shady lots featured low wrought-iron fences, azaleas, crepe myrtles, magnolias, and columned homes. Mockingbirds darted across well-kept patches of grass, seeking their insect prey.

Before growing into a pre-teen, I had spent many hours in our house's fenced and hedged backyard where I built forts and waged war on fire ants with a magnifying glass. Mom liked to sit reading a book in a lawn chair where she could watch me. Sandy soil composes most of Mobile's ground. Mom designated one corner of the yard as "the sandbox." Gradually, Ruthie—our Labrador retriever—and I extended the sandbox to include the entire backyard. Nobody could dig holes like Ruthie. Whenever I played in the sandy dirt, Mom encouraged me to go swimming afterwards. Dad had blown up my own swimming pool with a little air pump and then placed it in a sunny spot. Mom filled the pool with the house hose and let the sun warm it. Unlike the inside bathtub, she let me splash out as much water as I wanted. Ruthie liked getting into the pool with me. But as a fourteen-year-old, our house, yard, and neighborhood had become hopelessly boring.

Some accompanying Mom to meetings of parents and teachers couldn't be avoided. I hated being dragged around to different schools and meetings. But I did meet some interesting people. During one of Mom's meetings, a sight perplexed me. A boy and a girl—one brown, the other black—stood with two large white parents. I must have stared because the mother saw me watching and approached. The woman introduced herself as Mrs. Nancy Hobbs and asked, "What's your name?"

"Jeremy Parker."

Her husband had followed to stand by her. "Are you Katie Parker's son, Jeremy?"

The always-safe answer in south Alabama is "Yes, sir," and I used it.

"Jeremy, what do you want to be when you grow up?" Mr. Hobbs asked.

I remembered a joke to answer that tedious question. Boys at my middle school liked to banter it around. My father had called the joke disrespectful. But Dad wasn't around to hear. "An adult," I answered.

Both Hobbses belly-laughed loudly. "That was a good one," said Mr. Hobbs as he reached out to pat my shoulder. "Here, tell Oliver." He waved the brown-skinned kid over and repeated, "Jeremy, what do you want to be when you grow up?"

"An adult."

Oliver laughed with the Hobbses. "That's funny." Then he scurried off. I later heard him trying the joke on other people.

"May God bless you, Jeremy," said Mrs. Hobbs as they moved away. I liked the Hobbses.

Afterwards as Mom's meeting dragged on, I pondered Mr. Hobbs' question. What did I want to be when I grew up? Not like Mom and Dad, of course. But what?

I remember Mom getting a phone call that fall and then crying. Her mother, Grandmother McDougall, had been diagnosed with stage five breast cancer. She wasn't called Granny or Grandma, but Grandmother. She made my parents seem up-to-date and modern. Her husband, Mom's father, had died of a heart attack in his early fifties. And Dad's parents had been killed in a car accident before my birth. So I had only one grandparent living. Grandmother had doted on me. "You're so handsome. I pity the girls when you grow up."

I was the only boy Grandmother had, unless you counted the hundreds of boys she had taught in second grade. "I always wanted to have a little boy of my own," she explained.

Grandmother wanted to spend her last days and die at her home in Panama City, Florida. Mom went to care for her, leaving Dad and me in Mobile. Dad tried hard. He really did. But the house didn't seem like home without Mom. And all Dad usually had time and energy to cook was scrambled eggs.

At Christmas, Dad drove himself and me to Panama City in his pickup truck. I had visited Grandmother McDougall's home in Panama City many times. Unlike Mom and Dad's big house in Mobile, Grandmother's small tract house had been built of cinder blocks in the 1950s. She cared for year-round flower gardens and had a little Scottish terrier to keep her company. A lot of Auburn memorabilia decorated her home. Grandfather McDougall—although only a high-school graduate—had become an Auburn fan when he attended some special courses in forestry there.

I carried my bag into Grandmother's house. Mom and Dad greeted each other warmly. Mom started to tear up a little. Dad hugged her. Mom hugged me. "I've missed you, Jeremy," she said. "Has your father been taking good care of you?"

I started to bring up the steady diet of scrambled eggs but decided not to. Grandmother's house smelled badly—like medicine. I didn't bring that up either.

"Come with me now," Mom told me. She led me to Grandmother's bedroom. Putting her two hands on my shoulders, Mom guided me to Grandmother's bedside. The little Scottish terrier, McTavish, rested there on the bed next to Grandmother. His little black eyes stared suspiciously at me. The woman lying there seemed like a stranger: thin, most of her hair gone, eyes unfocused. Seeing her that way hurt. I looked down for a moment.

"Ah, Jeremy. There's my boy. The only little boy I'll ever have. The family legacy is yours to carry on now." I raised my head to see Grandmother's brown eyes focused as she admired me.

On Christmas morning, Mom helped Grandmother to an easy chair in her living room. Covered with a blanket, she watched us open our gifts. Mom had wrapped about a dozen presents for Grandmother to give me. After opening the first two packages, I discovered a pattern. All of Grandfather McDougall's Auburn University memorabilia that had decorated Grandmother's home had been bequeathed to me. To Dad, Grandmother gave all of Grandfather's tools. To Mom, she gave lots of keepsakes.

For Christmas dinner, Mom made a ham, mashed sweet potatoes, cranberry sauce, biscuits, and ambrosia made of oranges, shredded coconut, canned pineapple, and pecans. The Parker family being Creoles—that is, part Cajun—Christmas for us had always involved a bonfire and spicy seafood dishes with crawfish. To Dad I whispered, "Are we going to have a bonfire? What about the Cajun food?"

"Next year, Son," he whispered back.

We all sat at the big table in the dining room using Grandmother's best china. Dad usually thanked God for our meals before eating. On this occasion, Grandmother suggested,

"Let's let Jeremy say grace." Mom and Dad nodded and looked at me. Then we all bowed our heads.

Fortunately, I'd learned a prayer from the boys at school. "We thank you Father, Son, and Holy Ghost. Whoever eats the fastest gets the most." I looked up. Mom and Dad didn't even smile. But Grandmother threw her head back and laughed out loud. Then she said, "Pass your plate for some ham, Jeremy." Grandmother wasn't a Cajun or as religious as Mom and Dad either.

* * *

The day after Christmas, Dad and I traveled back to Mobile, leaving Mom in Panama City to care for Grandmother. Riding in the truck, I thought about death for the first time. Not mine, of course. Seventy or more years ahead sounded like eternity to me. I missed Grandmother already and speculated that Mom and Dad's deaths were forthcoming, too. I thought about Grandmother's words about our family's legacy depending on me.

"I prompted Dad with, "Why do Parkers eat crawfish instead of ham on Christmas?"

"That's because of your great-grandmother on my side. Her last name was Gaudet before she became a Parker."

I wondered why a name change led to my eating crawfish rather than ham, but knew enough by that age to wait Dad out.

Chapter Two

* * *

I didn't need to wait long. Dad always enjoyed reminiscing about any aspect of history. "You see, your great-grandmother grew up in a French family of fishermen in Louisiana. Her brother was Great-Grandfather Parker's best friend in World War I. After the war, she married your great-grandfather and left her Louisiana home. But she brought her family's traditions to Mobile with her."

"French people live in Louisiana?" I inserted.

"I should have said descendants of French people. In the late 1700s, the British wanted to own Canada and not Louisiana. They forcibly moved a lot of French settlers from Nova Scotia—called Acadia then—to Louisiana. The people ate whatever they could catch to survive and developed a taste for crawfish, which are now a special treat. Those people became known as Cajuns. Because of your great-grandmother, you're part Cajun yourself."

"Where did the Parkers come from before my great-grandmother made us part Cajun?"

"They came from England to North Carolina originally. Then the Parkers in America crossed the Appalachian Mountains in the footsteps of Daniel Boone." I had heard about Daniel Boone in school. I'll give you the short version of Dad's story:

The Boone-followers liked to fight. Dad described vicious battles the Parkers had with Indians on the frontier, which became Tennessee. He told me how Tennessee Parkers then crossed back over the mountains with other volunteers to defeat the British in the American Revolution at a battle called Kings Mountain.

Later some unfriendly Creek Indians–called Red Sticks–massacred a lot of settlers in south Alabama at a place called Fort Mims. To help the Alabamians, Andrew Jackson brought a group of Tennessee volunteers, including Daniel Parker, to south Alabama. Before finding the Indians, General Jackson used the riverside frontier town of Blakeley as his headquarters. Daniel really liked south Alabama and Mobile Bay. After defeating the Red Sticks at the Battle of Horseshoe Bend, the Tennessee volunteers beat the British again at the Battle of New Orleans. After fighting in those battles my great-something grandfather, Daniel, returned to Mobile Bay and became a fisherman. Parkers had lived here ever since.

That didn't stop Parkers from being in wars, though. Parkers could not seem to stay out of wars. According to Dad, a Parker related to me had fought in every war–except for the Parkers who lived in Mobile when the Tennessee volunteers went to

Texas to fight Mexicans in the Alamo. I had learned in school about the Alamo. All the Americans died there. I felt glad my fore-grandfather had been late to that party.

Dad went on, "Your job as a Parker, Jeremy, is to carry on the family for future generations of Parkers."

"Does that mean I have to fight in a war?"

"Your grandfather and great-grandfather did. One Parker, Ezekiel, fought for the Confederacy in the battle of Mobile Bay. But I didn't fight in any wars," answered Dad. "I certainly hope you'll never need to fight a war either. Wars change people, even if they aren't killed."

Between Christmas and the new year, Dad and I had fun together watching football on TV and going places around Mobile. I never got tired of visiting the battleship Alabama and looking at all the neat military stuff they kept in that park. Dad let me help him make seafood gumbo. With Ruthie, we took some long hikes on trails around the bay.

But January meant the beginning of Dad's busiest time for accountants—tax season. Ruthie and I saw less and less of him until I felt like an orphan. With Mom in Panama City and Dad busy at his firm, Bayside Accounting, I walked or rode my bicycle most places. I had become what people call a latchkey kid. Brody Nelson—a hulk of a football prodigy and less than a friend—publicly suggested that nobody cared enough to drive me anywhere. Most days after school I warmed up a frozen dinner for supper and watched TV. I did my homework in a perfunctory manner, if at all. Dad always came home late and tired. Most mornings he had already left for work before I got up. Ruthie tried her best to be good company. Even she seemed lonely, though.

One morning Dad waited for me to get up. He smiled broadly like he always did when seeing me. As I ate some cold cereal, he made a proposal. "Do you remember Mr. And Mrs. Hobbs?" I did remember the Hobbses. They had laughed at my joke about being an adult. Now that I mostly took care of myself, becoming an adult didn't seem so funny to me.

Dad continued, "Mrs. Hobbs noticed you walking home alone from school. And she heard about your Mom caring for your grandmother. She's offered to let you hang out at their house after school. I asked your mother, who knows the Hobbses well. She said that would be okay. What do you think?"

Anything would be better than the boring life I lived. And after having seen Oliver with the Hobbses at Mom's meeting, I had recognized him in my grade at school. I cautiously answered Dad. "I could try it."

"Fine. Then here's the address. It's only a few blocks out of your way coming home. Just get home before dark, okay?"

I took the paper on which Dad had written the address. Walking and biking as much as I did, I knew the area well. Finding the house wouldn't be any problem. "Okay."

"Now, Jeremy," Dad continued, "none of your pranks at the Hobbses'. You'll be a guest there."

"What pranks?"

"Remember taking all the labels off your mother's canned goods? One time you epoxied a quarter to the sidewalk and then videoed people trying to pick it up. Later you collected the numbers to pay phones, then dialed them. When people answered, you acted like they'd called you. None of that stuff at the Hobbses'."

"Oh, yeah. I remember now."

That afternoon after school I found the Hobbses' home. Smaller and less well-maintained residences than where I lived filled their neighborhood. The Hobbses' house looked tired and drab. Even I could tell it needed paint and some repairs. Someone had taped cardboard in place of a broken window. Live oak trees draped with Spanish moss shaded Mom and Dad's house and wide centipede-grass front lawn. The Hobbses' house sat in the sun with weeds in the small yard showing bare spots where kids played. Other mostly run-down houses crowded in close on both sides.

I knocked on the front door. The same Mrs. Hobbs I remembered answered. She was a big woman and stout with graying hair collected into a bun. No one would have ever called her pretty. Most of all, Mrs. Hobbs was loud. "Jeremy! We've been expecting you." Several young kids peeked around her. "Come on in, honey." She waved for me to enter.

Inside the Hobbs home I found about half the space of Mom and Dad's house. But unlike home, no rooms had been restricted like Mom's formal living and dining rooms. The Hobbses used all the space available and needed every bit. I soon learned that Mr. and Mrs. Hobbs took care of a lot more kids than the brown and black two I had seen at Mom's meeting. A dozen or more kids of all ages pursued a variety of activities: watching TV, doing homework, playing with toys or any of several pet dogs and cats, talking on the phone, crying about some trouble. A couple of the older girls took care of the infants and toddlers in a happy, noisy chaos. If the house only had half the space of Mom and Dad's, it had ten times the noise. I remembered the *tic, tic, tic,* of Mom's grandfather clock in our quiet Parker home.

"Would you like something to eat, Jeremy?" To my nod, Mrs. Hobbs pointed to a table with a lot of cardboard cartons. "Help yourself, honey." Then she reached out and grabbed Oliver as he watched us. "Oliver, you get Jeremy something to eat and show him around, ya hear?"

"Wazzup?" Oliver said before leading me to the table where I found a stack of paper plates, paper cups, and some plastic utensils. Gallons of sugar-sweet iced tea waited. In the cardboard containers, I found a variety of country-style foods: fried chicken and catfish, green beans, macaroni and cheese, mashed potatoes, biscuits, and Cajun-style dirty rice. Later I learned that Mr. Hobbs owned a nearby storefront buffet restaurant and catering business called The Full Plate. Three times a day he replaced the food on his buffet and sent the leftovers home.

Foods at the Hobbses' always came out of sync with the clock. For example, breakfast foods like eggs, sausage, and grits arrived for lunch. Lunchtime foods arrived for supper. Breakfast featured roast beef and roasted potatoes from the previous night's buffet. Near suppertime, I looked at the lunch spread. All the food looked better to eat than the health-conscious meals Mom served. After eating, I found plenty of fun stuff to do and plenty of boisterous company to join me doing it.

Everybody called Mr. and Mrs. Hobbs "Momma and Poppa." They were both too big to be called Mom and Dad. Those names seemed more appropriate for skinny, reserved parents like mine. Momma managed the Hobbs household with only a few rules: *no hitting, no lying, everybody pitches in, Momma's word on anything is final.* Momma herself went everywhere dispensing justice, assigning tasks, making sure all had reasonably clean clothes to wear and plenty to eat.

Momma knew who she wanted to be—a nurturer. She couldn't afford time to coddle, though. One afternoon, I scraped my knee playing outside. A silver-dollar-sized strawberry. I ran to Momma. "Ha!" she said. "That's only skin deep. Come to me when you need stitches." I really missed my own mother, who would have doctored my wound and offered heart-felt sympathy.

Poppa knew who he wanted to be, too—a chef and restaurant owner. He did all the cooking for the Hobbs clan through the leftovers he sent home, and, when necessary, by using the home grill. Like Momma, he tended stout and stood just a little taller than her. Poppa was the friendliest, most jovial person I ever met—a bald Santa Claus in an apron. He knew everybody. Or knew them a few minutes after they entered his eating establishment. Poppa liked everybody and everybody liked him.

Both he and Momma had come from farm country in Mississippi. Most of all they loved kids, regardless of their gender, age, or color.

What did I want to be? Just less bored and lonely right then. I started hanging out at the Hobbses' every day after school. On weekends I walked over, frequently taking Ruthie along. She loved the hubbub as much as I did. At home, Mom and I had read books like *Huckleberry Finn* and *The Grapes of Wrath.* At the Hobbses', we read Marvel and DC comics. At our house, I watched football with Dad and ice skating with Mom on a flat-screen TV. The Hobbses' older model tube TV showed professional wrestling whenever it came on. The Parker house computer was dedicated to homework. At the Hobbses', I never saw a computer, only a PlayStation 2 for video games. You get the idea. I reveled in the Hobbs experience.

Some days Oliver and I visited Poppa's restaurant. It had long collapsible tables–the same type our church used in the fellowship hall–and folding chairs. Like the Hobbses' home, the restaurant had a lively atmosphere. In fact, at the restaurant I found a lot of the same people as at the Hobbses' home: the older kids bussing tables or cleaning dishes, the hungry ones eating, a few visiting with the patrons. Poppa's restaurant always offered the buffet. But customers could also order more expensive entrees like grilled shrimp on a skewer from a menu. On Saturdays, Poppa grilled mountains of barbecue ribs for customers and took home the leftovers that night. On Sunday mornings, I walked to the Hobbses' early because before Momma went to bed on Saturday night, she always laid out the leftover ribs and other dinner foods in the kitchen as a breakfast buffet. The earliest risers would get their choices while Momma and Poppa slept in. The opportunity reminded me of my prayer at Grandmother's, except that at the Hobbses', whoever ate the soonest got the best rather than the most. Barbecue ribs on a Sunday morning became my all-time favorite breakfast. Ruthie loved chewing on the bones.

On Sundays Momma would eventually wake up about 9:00 a.m., drink some black coffee, and bellow, "All right! Y'all load up." Poppa and all the kids, including me, would immediately pile into a large passenger van. Whatever we were wearing at that time didn't matter. Looking into the van through the windows, you could see kids all squeezed together. Momma would drive everyone to the Pentecostal church.

Momma and Poppa were Christians like Mom and Dad. But their God seemed different from the one in my parents' Presbyterian church. Some kids called the church we attended "the frozen chosen." I didn't know what they meant by that. Those kids didn't know either. They only repeated what others had said. But our mostly boring church services *did* tend toward the somber. People at our church believed in a serious God. Their concept of God sounded a lot like Mom and Dad.

The Pentecostals' God acted less serious, livelier, and more fun. I found nothing frozen in that church. Kids ran up and down the aisles during services. Guitars, drums, and an old piano all accompanied the singing. And the Pentecostals sang loud.

The Pentecostal church reminded me of the Hobbses' home, a lot of noise and freedom of expression. It seemed like the

Hobbses brought home to church. Or maybe church to home. Either way involved a lot of commotion. Poppa's restaurant fit right in with church and home, making a tumultuous trio—Poppa himself being the loudest participant in any of the three places.

One thing I didn't understand about that church was that sometime during each service the preacher would shout, "Let's lift our praises to the Lord." Then a gentle murmuring would replace the noise and singing. Looking around I could see a lot of people with their eyes closed and their lips moving. Some would raise their arms toward heaven. Once I asked one of the older Hobbs girls what was happening. She answered, "They're speaking to God in tongues. Now you be respectful."

Momma's rule about everybody pitching in around the house also applied to me. I learned to do laundry and even wash dishes. One Saturday Momma placed a bundle in my arms while she dealt with another crisis. Her whole day involved jumping from one emergency to the next. "Hold him a few minutes, Jeremy."

I looked down to see the crying face of an African American baby. Police had dropped him off the previous night for temporary care. He became a foster child while his mother waited in jail for arraignment on a public drunkenness charge.

I'd never been responsible for a person before. Momma and the older girls dealt with crying babies by rocking them in their arms and cooing at them. Desperate for anything to stop the crying, I tried rocking and cooing like they might. To my surprise, that worked. The baby quieted and focused his little brown eyes on my face. When I inserted a finger into his tiny hand, he gripped my finger and continued to stare.

Chapter Three

* * *

"Give him this." Momma handed me a bottle of warm milk on her way to solve a different problem. As if I knew what to do with a bottle of milk and a baby. Maybe I didn't know, but the baby did. When I pushed the bottle's nipple into his little mouth, he began to suck.

After a while one of the older girls came by and burped him. She placed him back in my arms before moving on to a crisis of her own. First a blink, then another; in a minute the baby had fallen asleep.

I held the baby for two hours while he slept. Eventually Momma came to relieve me. After relinquishing the baby, suddenly I missed my own mother, especially her encouraging words. I looked up into Momma's face and asked, "Have I done okay with the baby, Momma?"

Momma looked down at me and smiled. "Nobody could have done any better, honey." Then Momma said, "I forget. You don't sleep here, do you? Thanks for your help, Jeremy. You best go on home now. Your father will be looking for you." But when I got home after dark, Dad wasn't home yet.

Ruthie, as always, wagged and jumped with joy to see me. I put a frozen pizza into the oven. Ruthie and I shared it on the couch. I remembered the day years ago when Mom had promised me a surprise. Dad drove us to a place with a lot of dogs mostly in fenced pens. The dogs barked and stood against the wire when we walked by. One of the black dogs, a Labrador retriever, had a litter of puppies.

"Pick one out, Jeremy," Mom had suggested. "We'll take it home."

How could I? They all looked the same–black, clumsy, and soft. The puppies stumbled around the small enclosure pestering their mother, wrestling among themselves, and chewing–above all, chewing. One girl puppy came over to chew on me. Her sharp puppy teeth hurt. But I didn't care. "This one," I had said. Ruthie and I fell asleep while the TV with the volume up played some silly movie.

Social workers took the foster baby I had fed at the Hobbses' away a few days later. I never learned what happened to him or how his life turned out. I pray for him sometimes, wherever he is.

* * *

I woke at dawn the next morning to the smell of frying sausages. *Mom must be home. Sweet,* I thought. But in the kitchen, I found Dad making a big breakfast for the two of us. His face lit up with that delighted smile he reserved just for me. "Good morning, Jeremy. What would you like to do today?"

"Isn't this Sunday?"

"Yes, but I hoped you would be willing to miss church today and try something fun with me."

"Sure."

Dad used his pickup and a trailer to pull his aluminum john boat to the river-tangled delta north of Mobile Bay. We used a ramp to back the boat into the Tensaw River. At first, we cast lures along the riverbank and caught a few yearling largemouth bass. Once the sun rose high, Dad anchored the boat near a huge tree that had toppled into the water. Using earthworms, we caught a bunch of hand-sized brim and a few crappies.

Of course, along with amateur historian Dad also came Parker stories while we fished. "Your ancestors lived north of the town of Blakeley." He pointed toward a woodsy section of riverbank. "That's where the town was before people deserted it in the 1840s because of yellow fever epidemics. The Parkers built their own boats. Your great-something-grandfather, Daniel Parker, made a dugout canoe from a single huge cypress tree he had felled upstream from here. Later he cut boards by hand out of a big live oak tree to make a flat-bottom boat. Like this one, only wood." He indicated the john boat. "They're useful in snag-filled water because they can pass over obstacles."

For once, I found these stories fascinating. "What obstacles?" I asked.

"Sandbars in the rivers or downed trees and vegetation in the swamps and bayous. The boats they built didn't have enough freeboard to venture into the bay, though."

"What could they catch in the rivers and swamps?"

"Well, fish, mostly using trot lines or traps. Also turtles. And alligators."

Dad mentioning alligators piqued my interest. "How did they catch the gators?"

"Mostly with a big hook and a piece of meat. Then from a boat they'd pull the gator to the surface of the water and shoot it in the head with a gun."

"That sounds mean."

"Maybe. But the people were trying to make a living, feed their families. There's a lot of meat on an alligator, especially in the tail. Then selling the hide brought in cash to buy things they needed."

Dad didn't speak for a while. I thought about my forefathers catching alligators. Dad soon started talking again, as I had anticipated he would.

"Eventually Parkers built more sturdy boats using lumber from a steam-engine-powered sawmill. Then they could fish the bay, especially collecting oysters. They sold those to rich people in Mobile. The Parkers never fished commercially in the ocean, though. That needs a bigger boat for when the water gets rough."

"Did Grandfather have a boat?"

"Your grandfather wasn't a professional fisherman. Too many men trying to make a living, especially in the Depression, had depleted the waters. My father worked in a paper mill. But he had inherited a wooden boat hand-made by your great-grandfather. He took me fishing in the bay a lot when I was growing up. In very calm weather, we'd go a little way into the gulf to catch snappers or mackerels."

"What happened to Grandfather Parker's wooden boat?"

"It got old and wasn't seaworthy, not even bay-worthy, anymore. After he and your grandmother died in the automobile accident, I donated the old boat to be sunk offshore in an artificial reef. Maybe someday we'll get an ocean-worthy boat and fish over the reef."

As the sun set, Dad and I went home to an empty house together. We fried some of the fish we'd caught for a stomach-extending supper.

That night I heard Dad crying out in his sleep without anyone to rescue him from a bad dream. He missed and needed Mom, too. I knew Dad had bad dreams now and then, but I didn't know why. He didn't like to talk about them.

* * *

One afternoon I lay on the floor at the Hobbses' reading comic books. The phone rang. "Somebody answer that!" Momma shouted from where she was helping one of the newer foster kids select something to wear from the vast wardrobe of used clothes the Hobbses kept.

I stood and picked up the phone. "This is an automated reminder," I heard. "You have thirteen days remaining to pay the balance on your loan before home foreclosure."

I went to where Momma stood with a girl about my age admiring her bright new dress in a cracked full-length mirror. "It's yours to keep, honey," Momma told her.

I repeated the phone call to Momma and asked, "What's a home foreclosure?"

Momma sighed deeply and answered, "Don't you worry about that, honey. The Lord takes care of his children."

The message had sounded ominous to me no matter what Momma said. I lay awake that night worrying about the Hobbses. I remembered when Grandmother McDougall had once said, "The Lord helps those who help themselves." To myself I added, *Or the Lord helps his children through someone else.*

After school the next day, instead of going to the Hobbses', I walked three miles to downtown Mobile and found my Dad's accounting firm in a single-story former residence on

Government Street. Inside, a lady sat at the front desk. I had met Ms. Goldstein before. She immediately recognized me. "Jeremy, are you here to see your father?" I nodded. She pushed an intercom button and leaned slightly toward it to speak. "Dave, your most important client is here to see you."

Dad's voice came back. "Send him in, please."

Ms. Goldstein opened a door and took me to Dad's office. There files had been stacked high on the floor, and piles of papers cluttered his desk and a nearby table. Dad had three computers. I thought, *This is why Dad has an office downtown. Mom would never let him get away with this mess at home.*

Dad stood behind his desk waiting for his most important client. When he saw me, his face lit up like it always did. This time some puzzlement mixed with his joy at seeing me.

"Jeremy, this is an honor." Then he thought a second. "What's the problem?" He knew that I understood not to bother him at the office during tax season except in an emergency.

I told him about the phone call I had taken at the Hobbses'. "What's a home foreclosure?" I asked. "It's bad, isn't it?"

"Yes, a foreclosure is bad. That's when people don't have money and creditors take their house."

The thought of the Hobbses without a house terrified me. "Can you help them, Dad, please?"

Chapter Four

* * *

Dad glanced at the stacks of files and piles of papers around his office. Then he looked back at me. He punched a button on his desk. "Dorothy, would you find me the phone number of The Full Plate Restaurant? I think they're over on Walnut Avenue. Our most important client has a concern."

Dad sat down behind his desk and motioned for me to sit in one of several deeply padded leather chairs. "How was school today, Son?" We chatted for a minute or two until Ms. Goldstein came in with a slip of paper.

Dad took the paper, thanked her, and dialed the phone. "Mr. Hobbs, this is David Parker over at Bayside Accounting." Dad listened. "Thank you, Tom. Please call me Dave. And I thank you for helping me take care of Jeremy during Katie's absence."

Just then Dorothy came onto the intercom. "Dave, the bookkeepers from the Value Pharmacy chain of stores are here." I knew that Value Pharmacy was one of Dad's biggest clients.

Dad put his hand over the phone's receiver. "Tell them something urgent has come up. I'll be with them in a few minutes. Serve them coffee and pastries in the conference room."

Dad returned to his call with Poppa. "So Tom, I heard a rumor that you're in some financial trouble. I don't mean to pry, but would you be willing to tell me about it?"

Dad listened for a while. Then he winced and summarized, "So the local banks turned you down for a loan to start your restaurant? Then you went to an alternative loan source, paid some substantial up-front fees, and signed a confess judgment agreement using your house as collateral? A year later the loan source wanted to raise the interest rate. When you objected, they called the loan and kept the up-front fees?"

Dad listened some more before saying, "Tom, I can't help you with the confess judgment. And don't bother hiring an attorney. The courts won't even hear your case, and they'll force the foreclosure on your home. The up-front fees you paid are gone forever. But maybe I could help you get a new loan, this time from a legitimate bank."

Dad listened again. "No, there won't be any charge from Bayside Accounting. An admirer of yours has retained our services on your behalf. If you could come in here tomorrow and bring your business books and your personal financial records, I could look at them. I can't make any promises, except to try."

After a pause, Dad finished, "Okay, Tom, see you tomorrow at nine. You're welcome."

Dad hung up and looked at me. "I'll try to help the Hobbses, Son."

"What's a confess judgment agreement?"

"That's when a person gives up their legal rights in return for something. Some people who have poor credit do that trying to borrow money. They think if they make all the payments on time, they'll be okay. Not always."

I didn't understand but nodded. Dad continued, "Son, there's nothing I'd rather do than spend the afternoon with you. But my biggest client has a major tax problem I need to solve. I'll see you at home tonight."

I took that as asking me to leave. And so I did. But I went away with a lighter heart knowing my father would help the Hobbses. I didn't see Dad that night, though. Ruthie and I had fallen asleep on the couch before he got home.

* * *

A week later I was outside playing a game of tag involving tackling with the Hobbs kids when Poppa came home unexpectedly. He wore his best suit. "Nancy, Nancy!" he shouted before he could even get in the house. Momma met him on their porch with an alarmed look. "We got a loan from a real bank. And at a lower interest rate! Dave Parker created a business plan for us. He set up a new bookkeeping system. Then he went with me to the bank to explain everything. He personally co-signed for one hundred thousand dollars. He said it was for his most important client."

Me and the other kids watched while Momma and Poppa hugged and cried. All of us ran to join the celebration. I'll always remember the crushing bear hugs both Momma and Poppa gave me. Poppa quickly changed into his cooking clothes and hurried to the restaurant to serve the dinner customers. Momma disappeared for a while to thank God in private, probably in tongues. All the kids wondered what had happened. I knew but didn't tell them anything.

* * *

That night over our scrambled egg supper, I asked Dad about what he had done.

"We just helped Mr. Hobbs organize his financial accounts in a manner the bank would appreciate. Mr. Hobbs is a great chef and personality, but not a very good bookkeeper. That's why the bank turned down his original loan application. Then Mr. Hobbs turned to a disreputable loan operation to get the money he needed to start his restaurant. Because he had signed a confess judgment agreement, he had no choice but to give his creditor all the money back when they told him to. Since he had already invested that money in the restaurant, then they were going to take his house, which he had used as collateral."

None of this made much sense to me. But I picked up on one important thing. "Accounting can really help people, can't it, Dad?"

"What we do is free people who might be poor in math to pursue their dreams."

"Thanks, Dad."

"You'll always be my most important client, Jeremy."

Dad didn't say anything about the co-signing. But The Full Plate Restaurant soon became famous in Mobile and attracted more customers than they could handle. Mr. Hobbs paid off the first bank loan early and started looking for other bigger places to start Full Plate Restaurants in south Alabama.

After nearly six months of loving care from Mom, Grandmother McDougall died. Nobody had to tell me that I was bad for feeling glad. Dad, and probably Mom too, may have felt some relief. But I felt glad.

Mom and Dad buried her next to Grandfather McDougall in Panama City. Grandmother's was the first funeral I ever attended of somebody I had loved. Then I did feel sad. Grandmother had called me the only little boy she'd ever have. She was the only grandparent I would ever have. A friend of Grandmother's gave her little Scottie dog a home.

Dad and I both rejoiced for Mom to be coming home. But Mom hardly seemed like the same person when she came back to Mobile. The state of her household under Dad's and my care turned her sadness into anger. Or maybe anger at us allowed her to channel her grief into something she could act on. Mom immediately put me to work picking up stuff left lying about, stripping the beds for the linens to be washed, dusting, and mopping the tile floors. Dad found an excuse and disappeared to his office downtown.

That night I had already gone to bed when Dad came home. The sound of his pickup truck reassured me, for a few minutes. Then the sound of loud voices found its way upstairs and through my bedroom door. I eased open the door and crept to my customary snooping position in the shadows at the top of the stairs.

I heard Mom's voice. "This place is a pigpen. How could you let our son live like this?"

Dad came back with the strong tone I rarely heard him use. "Jeremy didn't seem to mind. And are you forgetting that you left us here alone for months?"

"You know that I had to take care of my mother! I'm all she had."

"I know that I offered to bring her to Mobile or pay for home care in Panama City."

Mom's anger seemed to intensify. "That wouldn't be the same and you know it!"

"Maybe not. But Jeremy and I did the best we could under difficult circumstances. And I had tax season."

"You and your stinking tax season. Like that's an excuse to let everything else go to hell."

"Try providing for a family and buying a home for them without diligent work. I have responsibilities. I can't just go away for six months, like you did, and expect Bayside Accounting to continue paying the bills."

"You've got partners to take up the slack in an emergency."

"A six-month emergency? During tax season? You've lost your mind."

Mom spoke more quietly, deliberately. "Dave, you're working too hard. You're consumed with work and the firm. You're never here for Jeremy."

"How about you? Away at school meetings or obsessing over so much perfection. Everything must be just so. Maybe that's a reason for me to *not* come home."

"We're talking about Jeremy," Mom said. I felt my stomach lurch.

"Fine then. You smother him."

Mom's voice rose again. "I smother Jeremy?"

Now Dad's voice took on a deliberate tone. "Jeremy is nearly fifteen now. He needs more freedom. No nitpicking. Less hovering."

"Freedom to you means letting him spend months at the Hobbses'. Do you want his best memories of growing up to be at the Hobbses'?"

"Do you? And I consulted with you before I accepted their help," Dad came back.

I tiptoed back to bed and quietly closed my door. The sound of muffled voices still came through. I couldn't fall asleep. For the first time, I realized that dull, doting parents who are happy together are better than noisy, fighting parents. I thought about my classmates with divorced parents. Mom and Dad were arguing about me. That made me the problem.

* * *

I had hoped Mom and Dad would have resolved their issue overnight. They hadn't. Dad skipped breakfast–mumbling something about a bite downtown. "Fine," answered Mom.

Days went by with Mom and Dad barely speaking. Dad left for the office early and came home late. Mom fussed around the house and started watching daytime TV. Only at night after they thought me asleep did Mom and Dad communicate–if arguing can be called communication.

I knew the issues. Dad's work and unavailability. Mom's long absence, fussiness, and volunteer activities. Both focused their arguments on how the other's deficiencies affected me. I didn't need to eavesdrop, but I couldn't help myself.

"I'm working for you and Jeremy," Dad insisted.

Mom came back, "I listen to that all the time. If you're going to be condescending, at least be right about it. You work because you like being the big accountant who has all the answers."

"Listen all the time? You're not here all the time. Ask Jeremy."

And so on.

A vague idea started forming in my mind. I could pass myself off as sixteen and get work on a shrimp boat in Bayou La Batre. That would remove Mom and Dad's problem. They wouldn't have anything to argue about. My parents would be together again, and everyone would be happy. I pictured myself surprising them by coming home bringing gifts for Christmas. For the first time—not the last—I purposed to forge a different path than the rut my parents had followed.

I waited until the house quietened. Mom and Dad had finally gone to bed. Using my camping flashlight, I filled my backpack with a few clothes, my toothbrush, a large map of the United States, and the eighteen dollars and fifty-seven cents I had saved for Fourth of July fireworks. Careful not to wake Ruthie in the backyard, I slipped out the front door. The lock's clicking behind me brought a feeling of finality.

Chapter Five

* * *

Dogs grow up faster than little boys. But once grown, dogs recognize the importance of children—human puppies. After Ruthie had grown from a puppy to a dog, I had found that I had two mothers. Ruthie barked whenever I got into mischief or endangered myself. Although I loved Ruthie, she could be a terrible tattletale. Climb one of the big oak trees in our backyard . . . *bark, bark, bark.* Try Dad's saw on the picnic table . . . *bark, bark, bark.* Whenever this happened, Mom always sided with the dog.

Therefore, fat chance of sneaking away from Ruthie as I left home. She sounded the alert, barking. I could only stop her before she aroused Mom and Dad by opening the gate to the backyard and bringing her along. At first, she pranced around excited to see me, eager for a nighttime adventure. Then Ruthie acted suspicious, looking back for Mom and Dad. She followed me down the street, though.

We hiked in the cool springtime air for a couple of miles. Whenever a car passed, I pulled Ruthie into the shadows to hide us. Having made the decision to strike out on my own had relaxed me. I began to feel sleepy. We passed a cardboard box from some large appliance discarded on the curb. I picked up the box and carried it to a wooded lot nearby. There we crawled inside. Ruthie lay down beside me as I arranged my backpack as a makeshift pillow. She didn't put her head down. I felt safe knowing that Ruthie would stand guard. And her warmth against the cool air helped me fall asleep.

* * *

The sun had risen high in the sky when I woke up. Ruthie still lay beside me, her head up and eyes open. I felt a little superior to the kids already at school for the day. Then hunger made me realize that I hadn't brought along anything to eat. Not even any water. Memories of food aplenty at the Hobbses' returned to me. *I can't leave without saying goodbye to Momma,* I told myself.

A thirty-minute walk brought Ruthie and me to the Hobbses'. The school-aged kids had all left for the day. I found Momma caring for a foster baby and the youngest kids by herself. Poppa had left to serve the breakfast crowd at his restaurant

"Why are you here, Jeremy?" asked Momma. "Isn't this a school day?" Her eyes noticed my backpack. She bit her lip. "Well, as long as you're here, you might as well have some breakfast. You know where to find it."

I helped myself to chicken and beans left over from Poppa's buffet the previous night. Before I could hardly start eating, Mom and Dad showed up in Mom's car. Ruthie showed her relief at seeing them by lying down and closing her eyes. "Thanks for calling, Nancy," Dad said to Momma.

My parents sat down on either side of me. Mom's voice sounded urgent. "What are you doing here, Jeremy?"

I couldn't reveal my true intentions. "I got hungry."

"You could have woken me up," started Mom. Then she saw Momma point at the backpack I had left in the corner.

Mom sat in stunned silence. Dad took a minute to summon some words. "Why did you think you needed to leave home, Son?"

I looked from Dad to Mom but didn't speak. "You can tell us anything, Jeremy," Dad added.

"I've heard you arguing. It's always all about me. I'm causing problems." I heard a slight gasp from Mom, but she didn't speak. Dad looked down at the floor.

Momma spoke first. "Jeremy's okay here with me, if you two need to talk anything over."

"Are you sure?" Mom asked.

"Of course. And y'all needn't go far." Momma waved toward their car. To me Momma said, "After you've finished your breakfast, you'll need to make yourself useful around here."

Mom and Dad looked at each other. Without a word, Dad tilted his head toward the car. Mom silently nodded. "We'll be right there in the car in case you need us, Jeremy," she said to me. Together they walked in silence to the car.

* * *

After I had eaten, Momma put me to work collecting the dirty laundry, picking up debris from a house full of kids, and taking out bags of trash. Frequently, I glanced with apprehension out the window at the car where Mom and Dad sat talking. At first, they seemed to be arguing. *Are they deciding to get a divorce?* Then I started seeing some nods from each one as the other spoke. *Looks like Mom and Dad are working out the terms of their split. Or maybe they've agreed to a punishment for me.* Finally, they both bowed their heads as if saying a prayer then looked up and hugged each other.

The car doors opened. They came toward where I sat in an old aluminum lawn chair, bottle feeding the newest foster baby. I looked up to hear whatever bad news they would deliver. Dad spoke first. "Jeremy, your mother and I would like to ask you to forgive us. I've let my work become the most important thing to me. I even convinced myself that I did it for you and your mother."

Mom's eyes appeared red from crying. "I haven't been a good mother the last few months. I should have found a way to help my own mother without abandoning both of you. And I need to loosen up."

I didn't know what to do or say. Then Dad spoke again, "Will you forgive us, Son?"

I nodded. Then Momma came to take the foster baby from me. "Thanks for your help, Jeremy. You best go with your parents now."

With Mom, Dad, and Ruthie I got into the car. Supposing that they would take me to school, I said, "I don't have my books."

"There's no school for you today, Jeremy," said Dad. "I'm taking the day off myself. Tomorrow we'll all claim to have been sick. Now where would you like to go and what would you like to do?"

In the surreal circumstances, I couldn't think of any answer. Mom relieved me of the obligation. "Let's all go look at boats." As Dad stared at her in astonishment, she continued, "You've always wanted an ocean-worthy boat, Dave. We all need something we can do as a family."

Dad looked at her in gratitude. "A great idea, sweetheart."

Dad's john boat could only be used in calm water. But any boat we looked at today could carry us into the Gulf of Mexico and would have its own permanent home at a marina dock. Dad guided us toward a fiberglass cabin cruiser. Mom liked that idea because those boats included a tiny head with a toilet. We all enjoyed crawling over the boats and imagining ourselves on the ocean. Seeing Mom and Dad together and excited made me happy. We settled on a used cabin cruiser.

Everything changed for the Parker family after that day. In addition to buying the boat, Mom typed up a list of things she and Dad had agreed on. For a week or two, they both amended and eventually signed the paper. Dad made a copy and hung it in his office. Sometimes during school hours Mom and Dad went out to lunch together. They remained hopelessly old-fashioned. But they became a lot more fun even as fossils. Dad spent less time at his office. Mom planned day and overnight family activities. Most of all we used the boat. In the more difficult years ahead, the boat would become our safe place. Mom, Dad, Ruthie, and I could always be a family on the boat.

The first excursion into the gulf on our new boat made me seasick. Mom threw up, too. Not Dad. He must have had a perpetually empty stomach. Later Mom told me that he had been a little sick himself but tried hard to not show it. I caught my first red snapper that day.

Collecting oysters in the relatively calm bay didn't make me sick. Dad let me eat some oysters raw. Eating oysters made me feel grown up like Dad. Mom wouldn't eat any oysters raw. I guess because she was from up North, a Yankee. Mom did make the oysters into all kinds of wonderful cooked dishes. Her oyster stew had more oyster than cream.

In addition to fishing and collecting oysters, the boat enabled water skiing, exploring the inland waterways, and camping on barrier islands. Even working with lots of other boats to clean up floating trash on the bay was fun. Ruthie always loved going on the boat with us. The boat became like a member of the family.

For weeks, we kept up a lively dinner-time discussion about a name for the boat. I suggested naming it Gaines after the Confederate gunboat my great-something-grandfather Ezekiel used to fight the Yankees in the Battle of Mobile Bay. Mom proposed Mary, her deceased mother's name. Dad and I shook our heads toward each other when Mom looked away. Neither of us wanted any reminder of that grim time. Finally, we settled on Dad's idea—a name that sounded like a boat yet reflected his passion. I voted with Dad in gratitude of his helping Mr. Hobbs. The following Saturday, Mom and I held Dad's feet while he leaned over the side to stencil "Audit" on the boat's bow.

* * *

After we had Audit for a while, Dad asked me if I would like to invite any friends to go fishing. I invited Arthur and Sonny, who went to my school.

A few years earlier, Arthur, Sonny, and I had shared the sidelines on the same team in Mobile's ages 10-12 summer soccer league. There we had hoped to get into the game, run around the big grassy field, and kick at a ball—a big, soft ball that looked like it deserved kicking. Well, I happened to be small for my age. But accompanying that, I was also slow. Unless the ball somehow ricocheted directly at my feet, someone else always got to kick it first.

Arthur had about the same size and athleticism as me. Sonny—although bigger—wore glasses and tended toward the studious. He had the mistaken impression that soccer was a game. Brody Nelson knew different. Every sport was war to him. Kids on the opposing sides frequently left the field with split lips and bruised faces from Brody's elbows. So the three of us mostly watched Brody and our teammates chase the ball up and down the field. Time together on the bench nurtured our friendship.

When I did get in the game, Brody would usually knock me down, even though we played on the same team. Mom accused him of getting soccer confused with his other sport, junior football. Brody's parents insisted that being knocked down is part of every sport. Even after Mom switched my sport to tennis—no getting knocked down in tennis—my friendship with Arthur and Sonny remained.

A secret bond later sealed our friendship. That fall Brody had shared our sixth-grade classroom. There he acted just as insufferable as on the soccer field. Brody said that the girls in our class were so ugly that a frog wouldn't kiss them. He called the smaller boys like me grasshoppers.

The three of us resolved to do something to puncture Brody's balloon of arrogance. Over a couple of weeks, we gleefully argued scenarios among ourselves and perfected our plan.

Chapter Six

* * *

Like most students, Brody carried his books in a backpack. One day Arthur, Sonny, and I hurried back to the classroom after lunch in the school cafeteria. While my co-conspirators stood guard, I slipped a rubber snake into Brody's backpack.

The other pupils returned from lunch and our sixth-grade teacher, Ms. Hampstead, made us take our seats. Arthur, Sonny, and I glanced at each other in tense anticipation as Ms. Hampstead droned on about punctuation rules. I could hardly bear the suspense. Eventually, my heart leapt when she told us to take out our reading books. A loud girl-like scream pierced the room. Brody fled down the aisle between our desks, leaving the rubber snake lying among his discarded books.

Ms. Hampstead walked to Brody's place, leaned over, and picked up the rubber snake. The other kids laughed—all but Arthur, Sonny, and me. Fear of retribution if discovered as the culprits gave us previously unrealized self-control. Ms. Hampstead tested our self-control by lecturing the class about pranks. She pointed to Brody who, although shaken, had returned to his desk. "Look at poor Brody. Whoever did this has nearly frightened this boy to death."

Of course, her sympathy only heightened Brody's shame. I nearly drew blood biting my inner lip to avoid laughing out loud. Good thing. After school, Brody tried to find a stool pigeon among his classmates. He swore vengeance should he learn who had snaked him.

Arthur, Sonny, and I later met to take an oath of eternal secrecy. No one would *ever* know who had frightened "poor Brody." And when alone, any one of us three could simply say, "poor Brody" or "frightened this boy to death" to send us all into uncontrollable laughter.

In addition to Arthur and Sonny, I invited Oliver to go fishing on a calm Saturday. Dad let me steer Audit in tranquil Mobile Bay before reaching the gulf. As a fifteen-year-old, piloting a boat made me feel like a man. Being on the boat in the middle of the bay and so far from shore unnerved the three other boys. I remembered feeling a bit exposed and vulnerable myself on my first experience under the wide sky after living surrounded by tall trees and buildings in Mobile. Dad pointed to Oliver, the youngest. "When I was your age, my father took me fishing near here. He asked me to hold his best fishing rod and reel for a second while he got a Coca-Cola. Suddenly the rod just jumped from my hands and disappeared in the ocean. My father turned around to find me empty-handed."

"What happened to it, Mr. Parker?" asked Oliver.

Dad pantomimed losing the rod and exaggerated a surprised facial expression. "A big fish pulled the rod overboard. And might have pulled me in too, if it hadn't happened so quickly." Dad smiled as the kids relaxed. "But we won't let that happen to you." The boys laughed while Dad tied a cord to each rod and tethered it to a cleat on the boat.

Dad took us just a little way outside Mobile Bay. There we would try reef fishing on the old junk the state of Alabama had sunk to the bottom, possibly over Great-Grandfather's wooden boat. Because we had only three fishing rods, Dad let the three other guys fish first. Apparently, fish liked the junk on the bottom, because Oliver pulled up an eight-pound gag grouper.

That should have been my fish, I thought. Feeling cheated, I could hardly look at Oliver. Being so excited and happy, he didn't notice. Dad noticed, though. "These are our guests, Jeremy," he whispered. "You'll get lots more chances to catch fish than they will. Our job is to show them a good time."

I picked up on Dad's use of the words "our job." That made me his partner in taking the others fishing. After that, I hardly fished that day, only helped Dad. That night I heard Dad telling Mom, "I was never so proud of my son."

"Our son," Mom corrected.

The next week Oliver told all the kids at school about what a cool father I had. Even though Oliver lived at the Hobbses', I knew he wasn't their birth son but a foster kid like many there.

He didn't have a father of his own like I did. I got a strange feeling. Dad had told Mom about his pride in me, but I felt prouder of him.

* * *

In addition to buying a boat, Mom and Dad had also decided they wanted their marriage to be different. Change for them involved joining some discussion groups about marriage through our church. People from the church sometimes met at our house. Mom had long ago painted over where I had once created a crayon mural in the living room. I could still see a vague outline, but probably Mom and Dad's guests couldn't. Nobody seemed to mind my listening while the adults talked about loving and respecting each other. And the group members laughed a lot and enjoyed each other's company. I couldn't believe these were the same people we went to church with. The discussion groups had unfrozen the chosen.

Our church building loomed large and impressive with ornate brickwork, a vaulted ceiling, gothic windows, and stained glass. The Hobbses' church reminded me of their home. I later asked Dad why our church and the Hobbses' church worshiped so differently. He answered, "People conduct churches differently so everyone can feel welcome someplace. A lot of people from our church wouldn't feel comfortable at the Hobbses' church, and vice-versa. Your mother and I like our church because the traditions remind us to be faithful to God. We'd like you to attend with us as a family for a few more years, please. Then you can select any church you like."

Mom and Dad had met each other as part of a Christian student group in college. After college, they attended church most Sundays plus participated in occasional social activities. A man at our church played the pipe organ loud, perhaps to drown out the unenthusiastic voices singing hymns.

Too bad about the pipe organ drowning the singing though, because Mom and Dad could sing. They had learned how in a student ministry at Auburn. Singing must have played a big role in being a Christian student. But their music sounded different from the dirge in our church. Occasionally I would hear Mom singing lightly or humming a tune from her college days. But when Mom and Dad sang together, they sounded like angels.

One song became my favorite. Dad would start low with his deep voice. "Sing alleluia to the Lord."

While he held "the Lord," Mom would copy him with her higher clear voice. They would repeat the phrase while both raising their tone.

Then Dad would maintain his highest voice. "Sing alleluia." While holding the last word, Mom would repeat him. They did that twice. And together they would finish a low, "Sing alleluia to the Lord."

More verses would follow with different words but with the same rising and lowering tones and complement of their male and female voices. Whenever they sang "Alleluia," I imagined Christians waiting to face the lions. The Christians I imagined sang sadly in melancholic defiance of their persecutors.

A couple of months after we got Audit, our church hired a cool youth pastor named Walter. He had graduated from a Bible college somewhere in Georgia. Walter had a skinny, shy, Georgian wife who talked even more southern than us kids from south Alabama. Although in his twenties, Walter acted sort of like a teenager. He played a guitar and taught us a lot of the same choruses they sang at the Hobbses' church. I asked him about Mom and Dad's song, "Alleluia," and hummed a little of the tune. They didn't sing that at the Hobbses' church. Maybe it was too slow and quiet. But Walter knew "Alleluia" and taught us that, too.

One Sunday Walter taught us about "a great cloud of witnesses," meaning people who had died. Apparently, all those pioneers and fishermen and soldiers and lumbermen Dad and Grandmother had talked about watched me constantly like ghosts. The thought of them watching made me look over my shoulder and shudder. But I was glad they couldn't tell Mom some of the things they had seen me do. How could I possibly live up to all the expectations of two families united in Mom and Dad?

* * *

The fishing expedition had cemented Oliver into our group. Arthur, Sonny, Oliver, and I met on a Saturday to attend a newly released action movie at the theater in a shopping mall. The movie featured a man and a woman with superpowers battling an evil mechanical monster that sought to enslave Earth. I had always loved action stories and freely injected myself into the hero's character. On this occasion, I hardly noticed the man or the monster. My eyes couldn't leave the beautiful and well-endowed woman who dressed in a skintight suit and fought using acrobatic feats. I regretted the end of the movie.

Since Arthur had birthday money to spend, after the movie we drifted to the food court. The movie must have affected my companions the same as me because I noticed Arthur and Sonny staring at some teenaged girls at a nearby table. Only Oliver seemed unaffected, so far at least.

Arthur surprised all of us, including himself, by saying, "That one is all right." With that statement he tipped us into adolescence.

Our heads turned to follow Arthur's gaze. A perky brunette about our age sat two tables over gabbing with three girlfriends. Her eyes flashed toward us before she immediately diverted them. She said something we couldn't hear, and all the girls laughed. One looked over her shoulder at us.

Sonny watched the girls over his soda cup to disguise staring. "I like the tall one."

I looked to see a gangly girl with a brownish-blond ponytail. "I'll take the little redhead," I contributed. That left the skinny one with her back to us for Oliver. But he didn't object.

The perky brunette glanced our way again as the girls stood to leave. As they walked away, Sonny's and my choices looked back at us for an instant.

Our first guy conversation about girls ensued. Arthur and Sonny expounded on various physical attributes and compared the girls at the food court to various movie starlets. Apparently even Oliver had noticed the heroine in the movie and emphasized a preference for women with nice smiles.

"How about you, Parker?" asked Arthur.

I shrugged. "My mother wants me to marry Evangeline."

"Who's Evangeline?"

I shook my head. "Not a real person. A tragic heroine in a long story about a Cajun girl written by a poet named Longfellow."

By then any story about those of the opposite sex interested my companions. "Cajuns are hot. How's the story go?" pressed Sonny.

I gave them the gist of Mom's retelling of Longfellow's long and mostly dull story. "A young man, Gabriel, and a young woman, Evangeline, loved each other a lot. But on their wedding day, British soldiers forced the French-speaking people—called Acadians—to leave their homes in eastern Canada. Gabriel and Evangeline became separated when the British moved the people to Louisiana. Evangeline spent her lifetime searching for Gabriel and eventually found him in Philadelphia. He still loved her, too, and they kissed. Then they both died. People buried them close to each other so they could be together forever."

"Why didn't the soldiers want the French people in Canada?" Oliver asked.

"Who knows?" I answered. "The point of the story is that true love lasts forever regardless of the difficulty. Mom believes the story of Evangeline and Gabriel sets an example. She tells me, 'That's the type of love you want to share someday, Jeremy.'"

"I'll truly love a girl who's hot," contributed Sonny.

"Me too," Arthur agreed.

"I'm all for hot," I returned. "But I'm hoping for a hot girl who truly loves me."

Chapter Seven

* * *

Mr. Hobbs' storefront restaurant remained very popular. A much larger waterfront restaurant in Gulf Shores–across the bay from Mobile and down by the ocean–had closed when the owner retired after a stroke. Dad helped Poppa and Momma to create a new business plan and get a bigger loan from the bank to reopen the Gulf Shores restaurant. The Hobbses moved their entire menagerie to live in a bigger house with a swimming pool within walking distance of the beach. Poppa hired a manager to run the storefront restaurant in Mobile. But people said that The Full Plate wasn't the same without Poppa himself.

Momma and Poppa along with Oliver had left, taking with them the hubbub I could experience at the Hobbses'. Part of me felt deflated. Mom suggested that I invite some more kids to go fishing. I invited Arthur and Sonny again. Then–thinking of Oliver–invited seven less-advantaged kids who likely had experienced troubles in their lives. On Saturdays, Dad and I took them three at a time out to fish the artificial reefs. He let me steer

Audit until we left the bay. After that, I helped the kids catch snappers, groupers, and a few triggerfish, generally showing them a good time on the water.

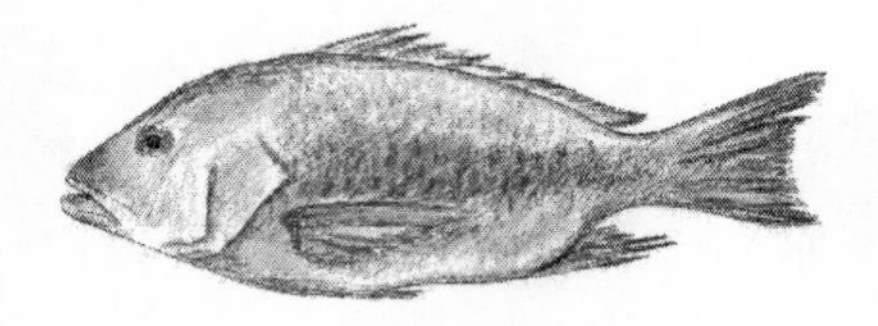

After one such fishing excursion, Mom said to me, "Your father and I are very proud of our son, you know."

On a Monday, one of the kids brought to school pictures of himself posed with the fish they had caught. Brody Nelson sneered at the pictures, calling the red snappers and groupers "minnows." The following day he produced a picture showing himself and a man called Hank standing next to a big tuna on a dock in the Bahamas. Brody called the kids that Dad and I had taken fishing "losers" and "bait fishermen."

I made a wild guess, "Did you catch that tuna yourself, Brody? Or did you pay Hank to let you take your picture with it? Are you jealous because they really *caught* fish?" Apparently, my jibe hit close to home. Because Brody–more than a head taller than me–pushed me down and called me a pathetic wimp. After that, he took every opportunity to deride me and those who'd gone fishing with us. Some of Brody's group did the same.

A few weeks later, I found myself alone in the school hallway after having served detention for chewing gum in class. I had prepared for such an opportunity. Pausing by Brody's locker, I slipped a rubber snake through his locker's vent.

* * *

Hurricane Katrina hit Louisiana and New Orleans near the beginning of my last year of middle school. The levees protecting the city from Lake Pontchartrain failed and flooded neighborhoods. With Mom and Dad, I watched pictures on TV of people wading through waist-deep water trying to find dry ground. Many of them carried children.

I thought about Mobile Bay and pointed at the TV screen. "That could happen to us, couldn't it?"

Mom saw the expression of fear on my face. "We could get hit by a hurricane, yes. But not flooded like New Orleans."

"Why not?"

"Half of New Orleans is below sea level, honey. Mobile is all above sea level. Lake Pontchartrain isn't really a lake. It's a brackish estuary connected to the Gulf of Mexico like Mobile Bay. So a storm surge from a hurricane can make the water level rise and put pressure on the levees. But the city being below Lake Pontchartrain is what has caused the disaster."

For once, Mom's science details interested me. "Why would they build a city below sea level?"

"Ask your father that."

Without being asked, Dad started, "Settlers built the original city on two long mounds—sort of like an ancient sand bar—created by the Mississippi River when the glaciers covering our northern states and Canada melted. Swamps and marshes just barely above the ocean at high tide surrounded the higher ground. But as the city grew, they needed more room. The people dug canals to drain the marshy land. When the ground that had always been wet dried out, it slowly sank."

Mom broke in with more science, "Jeremy, have you ever noticed how a wet sponge gets smaller when it dries out? Marshy ground acts the same way. Also, marshy ground contains a lot of organic material like dead water weeds. Without the swamp water, air decayed the organic material around New Orleans, letting the ground shrink even more."

Ground shrinking sounded incredible to me. "Then why didn't the water rush in as soon as the ground sank?"

Dad resumed the historical side of New Orleans' story. "The water tried. People built levees or dikes to keep the water out. But the levees also kept the river from replenishing the ground with sediments during floods. Over two hundred years the ground kept sinking and the people kept building the levees higher."

I looked back at the TV screen where a Red Cross phone number had been superimposed on the picture. "Wouldn't God want us to help them?"

Mom and Dad looked at each other. Dad nodded to Mom. "Sure, honey," she said and wrote a dollar amount on a piece of paper. Dad nodded again when he saw the figure. "Jeremy, why don't you call the number and make a donation? Here's a credit card to use."

I looked at the number Mom had written. It exceeded the total of all the allowances I would receive in five years. Making that call made me happy. My questions had resulted in helping people.

* * *

As an accomplished athlete in a jock-revering culture, Brody had found a wide group of admirers and followers at our middle school. Already some speculated on which college football scholarship he might eventually accept. Brody knew what he wanted to be—dominant over all others in every aspect of life. I realized what I wanted, too—to not be dominated by Brody.

Some new kids—refugees from Katrina—joined our classes. They acted uncertain, even scared, in a totally new place. Brody called them "newbies" and made a joke. "How can you tell if a kid is from New Orleans? Check to see if his feet are wet."

Most of the boys—especially Brody's admirers—laughed. I didn't laugh at all and went to sit by some of the new arrivals.

Brody noticed and followed me with a lot of kids trailing behind to watch what happened. "You're dripping on the floor, Parker."

Brody and the others laughed when I glanced down at the floor. I didn't see any water and looked up. Brody stood menacingly near, the others like a wall behind him. "I'm glad to see you sitting with your wet-foot friends," he said. "Do you feel nervous on dry land?"

Stung by the laughter I stood up and shouted, "Get lost, you big jerk!"

Brody stepped even closer. "What did you call me?"

I stood up to answer. "You're just a dumb jerk."

"So now you're calling me dumb?"

An insult popped into my head. "Yeah. If brains were dynamite, you wouldn't have enough to blow your own nose."

"That's big talk coming from a dweeb like you. You're so ugly that when you were born, they slapped your mother."

I didn't understand that, but it had something to do with somebody mistreating Mom. I reflexively clenched my fists.

Brody saw my reaction and laughed. "Ooooh. Your mother must be a wet-foot, too?"

A few weeks earlier I had seen a movie about a smaller boy being picked on by a bully. The boy knocked down the bully, who then turned out to be a coward at heart. In the movie, the other kids had congratulated and thanked the boy for standing up for all of them.

I lunged forward, pushing Brody in the chest with my two hands and my elbows locked. Unlike in the movie, Brody didn't topple over backwards and grovel in fear. In fact, I sort of bounced off him. He remained standing like a tree. Then I had an instantaneous impression of a flesh-colored blur before my eyes. I felt an explosion of pain in my nose as my head popped backwards and my body followed it.

On the floor I tried to figure out what had happened. The pain made thinking clearly impossible. As I started to get up, my legs felt too weak to support me. My eyes focused on shoes and legs standing around me. A sarcastic male voice, Brody's, said, "See what I meant. You're dripping on the floor." I looked down to see drops of blood falling from my nose onto the concrete. I heard laughter and saw the shoes and legs walk away.

One of the Katrina kids helped me to stand up. Another one offered me a napkin from his lunch bag. Using the napkin, I blocked the blood dripping from my nose.

"It's just you and me tonight," Mom said before dinner that night. "Your father went out to dinner with a new client."

I sat down at the table, glad that Dad wasn't home. He possibly would have guessed from my appearance that I had been in some sort of scuffle. "Do you have a cold, Jeremy?" Mom asked. "You seem congested. And your eyes look puffy and bruised."

"I'm okay."

She put her hand on my forehead. "Have you got a fever?"

I couldn't breathe through my nose and had a headache from Brody's punch. But I brushed her hand away. "I said I'm all right."

"Well, let me know if you feel sick." Mom went on to ask, "How do you like your new teachers?"

"They're okay."

"Jeremy honey, have you started thinking about what you might like to do after high school?"

Occupied with the headache, I snapped, "No." I continued trying to breathe in sullen silence.

"You know you're eligible for the PSAT next year. That's good practice for the real exam."

"I don't care."

"But you do plan to go to college, right?"

At that moment, I wanted to get as far away from Alabama and Brody as possible. "Maybe. But Mom, I want to see the country, the world."

"I could use a bit more travel myself. Your father has a strong attachment to this area. He feels safe in south Alabama. He belongs here. For me, no place without him is as good as being here with him."

"Sometimes I think Dad just wants me to carry on the Parker family tradition in Mobile. I don't want to be stuck here all my life."

"You won't be, honey. And your father will be happy, as long as you're happy." Mom sat thinking as if trying to decide something. "Having a Parker to carry on the family heritage was *very* important to your father's parents. I think your father sort of feels like he owes them that legacy. That's a lot like how I felt the necessity of caring for my mother in Panama City. But your father knows you need to have your own life."

"A dull life like Dad's?"

"Actually, he and I are not as dull as you might think." Mom smiled and went on to describe Auburn football games with friends, snow skiing in Colorado, attending Broadway plays in New York, camping on Cumberland Island National Seashore, and other adventures—all before I was born.

She shrugged a little. "Then, once you were born, Dave felt a tremendous responsibility to provide security and make a life for you. At about the same time, his years of excellent work started bringing lots of lucrative new clients to Bayside Accounting. He started working harder than ever and—as he'll tell you now—lost his head. I kind of lost my head working with the schools."

She reached out to pat my hand. "You'll have an exciting life, honey. I promise."

I'll make sure of that, I promised myself.

Chapter Eight

* * *

That winter a new brand of athletic shoe had become a must-have accessory for teenagers. All the guys my age wanted them. The most famous NBA players endorsed that brand. Any guy who didn't wear those shoes would be judged a loser by his peers. Brody had gotten the shoes before anyone and snubbed anyone who didn't wear them. I simply had to have those shoes.

Dad must have been a loser at my age. And Mom shared his loserness because she had married him. Neither of them understood the necessity of the $155 shoes.

"Jeremy, look how tall your father is," Mom attempted to convince me. "Now look in the mirror. See how lanky you are. You'll have a growth spurt soon. Those shoes won't fit you next year."

Dad chimed in, "They make those shoes in Vietnam for about one dollar each, Son. The rest is all advertising hype and celebrity endorsements. The same Vietnamese factories make shoes that retail without the logo for ten dollars."

I had to crush Mom and Dad with irrefutable logic. "All the other guys have them." Once I sensed them hesitate, I dropped the unanswerable clincher, "Don't you want me to be happy?"

Mom and Dad's eyes met. Mom raised her eyebrows and Dad shrugged a little. "Your sixteenth birthday is in a couple of months," Mom told me. "We'll buy you the shoes in advance. But that's your birthday present for this year." Dad gave his tight-lipped smile, meaning that he wouldn't disagree with her.

I felt such joy that I almost hugged Mom and Dad. But I caught myself. Guys my age just didn't do that.

I'll always remember pulling on those shoes and lacing them up. I felt like somebody. I knew people would treat me with respect.

* * *

Everybody knew about Zeek. He was a huge gator that hung around in a tidal creek that led to Mobile Bay. Former science teacher Mom suggested that Zeek was most likely a female gator and should be named Zina. Being male somehow made Zeek seem more formidable. Mom also disputed that. "A female alligator is the most dangerous, especially if you get near her nest."

Anyway, a week after getting my new shoes, I walked with Ruthie on the path that followed the creek. I spotted Zeek floating patiently near the "Do Not Feed the Alligators" sign. Somebody had marked out "the Alligators" and written "Zeek." That's how everybody knew his name. Standing by the "Do Not

Feed Zeek" sign, people would toss in table scraps, parts from cleaning fish, banana peels, Coco Puffs . . . Zeek would eat anything.

Gators' ability to lie or float totally motionless in the sun had always intrigued me. Mom had explained that the bumps on their backs had densely packed blood vessels and acted like a solar collector for a cold-blooded body. Whatever. *Maybe I can get Zeek to move,* I thought.

A short, thick stick lay on the ground nearby. I picked it up and threw it at Zeek. Immediately I heard a splash near my feet. Ruthie thought I had thrown the stick in the water for her to retrieve. Zeek didn't react to the stick. But seeing a dog swimming in his direction enlivened him considerably.

As Ruthie grabbed the stick and turned back, Zeek started to glide toward her. Ruthie headed toward me snorting and wagging her tail above the water. Zeek accelerated toward a meal that could last for days. I desperately looked around and saw nothing to distract the alligator. The only thing I had was the $155 shoes on my feet. I took off one of my new shoes. As Ruthie approached the bank, Zeek had come to within just a few feet of her hind leg. I threw the shoe directly in front of Zeek's nose. Instinctively the gator chomped on the shoe, giving Ruthie a few seconds to clamber up the bank with the stick. She brought the stick to me for another throw. I grabbed her collar and watched as Zeek chewed and swallowed my most prized possession.

I walked home wearing one shoe. Mom, who never missed anything, saw me limping up the driveway. She waited for dinnertime before inquiring. "How are your new shoes working out, Jeremy?"

Her tone told me that she already knew something had gone wrong.

"Uh, I lost one of them."

Mom acted surprised. "You lost one? How did you lose one?"

"I'd rather not say."

"Jeremy, I want to know how you lost one of those expensive shoes you wanted so badly."

I sat in sullen silence. "Hold on, sweetheart," Dad intervened. "A young man is entitled to some privacy." He turned to me. "Jeremy, did you do anything immoral or illegal losing your shoe?"

Dad hadn't included stupid. "No."

Dad spoke to Mom, "Then let's wait until Jeremy is ready to tell us, if ever."

Mom huffed a little but went along with Dad. I had to wear my old sneakers after that and got no additional gifts for my birthday.

A few months later I told Mom and Dad the story about what had happened with Zeek. They laughed out loud and didn't need to ask if I had learned a lesson about thinking before acting. Telling them also taught me that I could tell a good story.

Fishing reports promised that the king mackerel had started biting. Dad suggested that just our family go fishing. He always took inexperienced guests bottom fishing. Drifting over the reefs brought smaller fish but many more of them, and they were easier to land. Catching king mackerel meant trolling all day in the rougher water of the gulf. Mom declined our invitation to spend all day on a pitching boat. She claimed needing to catch up on some correspondence. We left Ruthie home to keep Mom company.

We left the marina at 5:00 a.m. and reached the prime fishing grounds off the coast by 7:00 a.m. Motoring out with the sun breaking the horizon in the east made me feel my own roots on the Gulf coast. I shook off that feeling. *I'm leaving here someday*, I promised myself.

Dad surprised me by asking me to steer while he watched the trolling rig. I had guided Audit in the bay on several occasions. I had never piloted in the ocean.

"You can see where we are relative to the reefs on the GPS map. Just stay within the boundaries and watch out for other boats," he told me. As I took the controls, I could feel the pride of my ancestors and hoped some did watch as the Bible verse had claimed. I had joined the long lineage of Parker boatmen. *You're leaving in a few years*, I reminded myself again.

"Look for and steer toward the greenish water," Dad called from the stern. The greenish water showed where the bay and ocean water mixed. Nutrients from the Alabama and Tombigbee Rivers fertilized the ocean's algae. Protozoa ate the algae. Little fish ate the protozoa. Bigger fish ate the little fish. I caught myself. *You're thinking just like Dad!*

We trolled for three hours. Dad had caught three respectable kings. He offered to steer while I fished. But I'd caught plenty of mackerels. This was my first time guiding a deep-sea fishing boat. I imagined the kids at school seeing me.

"Did you see that?" Dad shouted. I could hear excitement in his voice. I looked behind us. I had turned the boat to loop around for another pass near the reef. The whiplash effect around a curve forced the trolled mullet bait to the surface. A dark shape came up under the wake of our bait. A massive fin broke the surface.

"What is it?" I yelled back at Dad.

Before he could answer a dark bill emerged from the water and appeared to slash at the bait. Dad released the drag and let the mullet bait sink as if the fish's bill had stunned it. In a few seconds, the line went tight. Dad re-engaged the drag and jerked the rod tip above his head, setting the hook with all his strength. Immediately the reel screamed as the fish surged away, taking out line faster than I had ever seen.

I stopped the boat. "What is it?" I repeated. "A shark?"

"It's a sailfish," Dad grunted out as he desperately held onto the rod. Suddenly the sailfish leaped, twisting in the air seven or eight feet above the water. I had never seen anything so dramatic or so beautiful.

The big fish resumed its run. The reel screeched. Nearly all the line meant for a mere mackerel had already been taken out.

"Put the boat in reverse, Son. Chase the fish backwards," Dad ordered.

In my haste, I pushed the throttle the wrong way and started forward.

"The other way," Dad yelled.

In reverse, I backed the boat as fast as it would go toward the disappearing line. The line leaving the reel slowed. The sailfish came up again, thrashing on the surface, its long fin splashing water in both directions. After a moment the sailfish jumped vertically with its tail still at the water's surface. The rapid movement of its tail fins made the fish appear to walk across the surface of the water.

Suddenly the line went slack. "Did you lose him, Dad?"

"I don't think so. He's coming this way. Go forward now and run from him."

As I drove the boat forward, Dad started to reel in line the fish previously had taken out. The line went taut again, perpendicular to the direction we were traveling.

"Stop now!" he ordered.

I stopped the boat. The sailfish broke water again about a hundred yards from us. It jumped again and again and again. I silently asked God to give Dad that fish.

Gradually the jumps became lower, the fish's twisting less intense. Dad started pumping the sailfish toward the boat by raising the rod tip, then reeling in a few feet as he lowered it. After twenty more minutes of this, the exhausted sailfish glided alongside the boat.

Dad handed the rod to me. "Hold him, Jeremy." Just then the sailfish tried one last feeble thrust for freedom. I held on and followed Dad's example by pumping the fish thirty feet back until it was alongside us again.

I expected Dad to use the gaff. But he pulled on rubber gloves. He leaned over the transom, grabbed the sailfish's bill, and with a smooth motion pulled the eight-foot fish into the boat.

I'd never seen such a spectacular creature; the sunlight reflecting on the fish's scales made the fish seem to sparkle in pale silver, bronze, and violet colors. A purple top fin with black spots ran nearly the length of its body. Even with the fish's beauty, I started wondering how sailfish would taste.

Dad rustled in our on-board toolbox. With our biggest pair of pliers, he grabbed the shaft of the hook and twisted, forcing the barb to break through the surface of the fish's jaw. "Hand me the leader cutter," he said with a calm I could hardly believe. Using both hands on the cutter he cut off the barb. Then he easily pulled out the hook shank the same way it had entered.

Next, Dad grabbed our portable scale. While he weighed the

fish, he said, "Get the cell phone from the cabin." The scales read sixty-seven pounds. Dad held up the fish while I used the cell phone to tap several pictures from different angles. Then, to my surprise, Dad gently eased the magnificent fish back into the ocean. He held it in the water for an instant, savoring the moment, before releasing it. The sailfish lay still in the ocean, its gills barely moving, and rolled on its side for a second. *It's going to die,* I thought with dismay. The fish righted itself by a small flip of its tail fin. Then, with a slow swoosh of its entire body, the sailfish disappeared out of sight into the green water. The fish had been out of the ocean only four minutes. I said a little prayer thanking God for helping Dad catch that sailfish.

Dad sat down as exhausted as the fish. After a minute, he looked at me. "Thanks, Jeremy. I couldn't have caught it without your help. The three happiest things in my life have been marrying your mother, holding you the first time, and catching that fish."

Then I pondered, *A wife, son, and a magnificent fish. Are those enough to make a life worthwhile? Seems so to Dad. Can't I do better than that with my life? What would be better?* For the last, I had no answer.

Chapter Nine

* * *

Finally, my class reached tenth grade and started at West Side Senior High School. West Side's football coaches had watched Brody playing quarterback on our middle school's team. Diligent work in the weight room had transformed him into a hunk of bone and muscle. A punishing runner, Brody had developed the trick of lifting his knee into the face of a would-be leg tackler. Players on the opposing team lay hurt on the field during every game. Brody could also throw the ball with accuracy from the pocket or while rolling out.

Trouble was the coaches already had an experienced quarterback, a senior, for the coming season. They didn't want to waste a year of Brody's high school eligibility. They also reasoned that given another year to grow even larger and play quarterback on the middle school's team would make Brody a truly star player. He could enable West Side to defeat the dominant schools in Birmingham and Montgomery. The coaches promised Brody's parents that he'd have a better chance at a scholarship from a football powerhouse like the University of Alabama and a path to the NFL if he repeated ninth grade. They explained that Brody could be "redshirted" to achieve maximum potential. And so, Brody didn't go up a grade with our class. I didn't miss him one bit.

As for me, at age sixteen I achieved the teenage equivalent of finding the Holy Grail. I passed the driving test and got my driver's license. Then Dad bought a Toyota Corolla with 176,000 miles on it for $1,200. "This car is for local use only and still belongs to me," he said as he handed me the keys. With the keys he provided a credit card. "This is only for gas. Try to keep the car at least half full at all times."

Mom had something for me, too–a cell phone. Not a smartphone, just an ordinary cell phone. Most of the kids my age had gotten cell phones by then, but not all. "The new rule is that you'll keep this with you all the time, especially while driving," she explained. "Not answering any call from me will result in loss of the phone and the car." With the car and phone, I felt like I had won the lottery. I could finally be what I wanted most–not dependent on my parents. And yet, I also felt like a wild animal that has been radio tagged. Mom could call anytime she wanted just to know my location and what I might be doing.

The car allowed me to drive myself to West Side High. There I gratefully entered Brody-free tenth grade. Mom had re-engaged in programs to help Mobile's public schools. Neither of us wanted to return to the era where she had to chauffeur me around and haul me to her meetings. And as a bona-fide high school student, being picked up by my mother would be unthinkable. The freedom the car provided allowed me to dissociate from my fossilized parents regarding all things related to school. A bright new day had arrived.

* * *

"Aaah!" Dad's cry woke me in the night. Then I heard the familiar soothing tones from Mom.

The next morning after Dad had left for work, I finally asked Mom about his nighttime outcry.

Mom remained silent for a minute as if deciding how to answer. She sighed. "Your father cries out during nightmares. I remember the first time that happened after our wedding. He nearly scared me to death."

"Nightmares? What causes them?"

A few more moments of silence passed before Mom asked, "Did you know your father had a brother?"

"Dad had a brother? Why hasn't anyone ever mentioned him?"

"That's because he committed suicide. Your father found his body."

"What?"

Mom remained silent again. Our school had shown a video about the danger of teenage suicide. So I had heard the major causes. "Was Dad's brother depressed because of peer pressure? Did he feel like he couldn't measure up?"

Mom sat down on the sofa and signaled for me to sit down as well. "No. This happened before I met your father. But I'll tell you what his mother, your grandmother Parker, told me about a month after we had been married."

I waited for her to continue.

Mom spoke slowly and with difficulty while looking at the floor. "Twelve years separated your father and his older brother, Chuck. Dave's brother took ROTC at the University of South Alabama here in Mobile. After graduation, he received a commission as a lieutenant in the army. Chuck volunteered for the war in Vietnam. Something horrible happened on a patrol. As a green officer, he ordered his men into an ambush, I think. The enemy killed six of the men in your uncle's platoon and wounded several more severely. He blamed himself for being stupid and overly enthusiastic."

"Why would that give Dad nightmares?"

"In the months after the ambush, Chuck went crazy trying to make up for what happened. He killed a lot of Vietnamese who may or may not have been Viet Cong. The army quietly gave him a medical discharge.

"Your uncle came home haunted by the war and what he'd done. He needed counseling or at least somebody to listen to him. Your grandfather's generation never talked about their experiences in World War II. Your grandparents thought that talking would only make things worse for Chuck. In 1969, people in the US were much more likely to criticize Vietnam veterans than listen to them.

"The only one who would listen to Chuck was your father. He loved and respected his older brother and wanted to help him. Dave listened to all the gruesome details of the war. Your uncle even suggested that the Parkers have a violence demon lurking inside them. Later your uncle couldn't tolerate the memories and killed himself."

I sat transfixed and thought about all the wars Parkers had fought in.

Mom sat silent for a minute before continuing. "Your grandmother said that your father's nightmares started after that. He dreams himself doing terrible things." She then looked at me. "Have you ever noticed how your father can become totally fixated on details other people would consider tediously dull, like accounting or history? I think filling his head with details helps keep your father from thinking about the things his brother told him."

I asked Mom, "Do you think all the Parker men have a demon?"

She laughed for the first time. "No, I'm sure your father doesn't. He's too self-sacrificing and kind to have a demon. You, I'm not so sure of." She looked closely at me and then smiled. "But yours is a mischief demon, not a demon of violence."

Arthur's parents had transferred him to Mobile Academy, a private school, to attend senior high. And our teachers diverted studious Sonny into the honors track of classes. So I entered tenth grade classes without close friends. At lunch one day, I noticed a group of guys from a different middle school than I had attended laughing. I joined them to hear jokes directed at Auburn University.

"What do you get if you drive across Auburn's campus very slowly? A diploma."

"Know how to get an Auburn graduate off your porch? Pay for the pizza!"

"Did you hear that final exams are postponed at Auburn this spring? Too wet to plow."

I knew Mom and Dad had both attended Auburn but repeated some of the jokes over dinner anyway. They each smiled and laughed a little. Mom had a joke, too. "Did you hear the Auburn library burned down? The saddest part is that half the books weren't even colored in yet."

That *was* funny. Who would have expected that my mother could tell a joke?

Then Dad tried a joke. "Students from the Universities of Alabama, Auburn, Georgia, and Tennessee all climbed a mountain leading to a cliff. There they started arguing about who loved their school the most. The Tennessee man insisted that he was the most loyal. He yelled out, 'This is for Tennessee!' and jumped off the cliff. Not to be outdone, the Georgia man then shouted, 'This is for Georgia!' and jumped himself. Then the Auburn man yelled, 'This is for Alabama! ROLL TIDE ROLL!' and pushed the Alabama man off the mountain."

Mom laughed so hard that a tear ran down her cheek. Dad chuckled with her. Dad said, "I think it's about time we took Jeremy to a football game."

"Past time," she answered.

* * *

A few weeks later I found myself dressed in orange and riding in Mom's car toward Auburn. Dad parked in a big field packed with cars and RVs. Everybody started moving toward the huge stadium. A lot of people kept yelling, especially those dressed in purple from LSU. Inside the stadium, people wearing Auburn orange and LSU purple had already started shouting at each other. Two large bands played as loud as they could. I loved the commotion, and nobody, least of all Mom and Dad, cared how much noise I made. Dad found our places and tried to convince Mom that seats behind the end zone are a great place to watch a game.

Then a group of cheerleaders came running across the field carrying a giant blue and orange flag. Someone in a tiger costume frolicked in front of the crowd. A bald eagle flew down from somewhere high to sit on a perch on the sidelines. So much happened at once that I didn't know where to look. Next, Auburn's players wearing dark blue uniforms came running onto the field. The noise doubled. When the players wearing white and purple sneaked in, the purple-dressers in one part of the stadium attempted a cheer.

I'd watched plenty of football on TV and seen a few high school games. I knew well how the game worked. But in person in the big stadium, I had trouble understanding what was happening on the field. Sometimes nothing happened. All the players just stood around. Since Dad seemed distracted, I asked

Mom about that. “The referees called a time-out so the TV could show commercials,” she explained.

The game swung back and forth. I’d never seen so many adults acting crazy. Finally, the scoreboard read “Auburn 21: LSU 17” with about two minutes remaining in the game. After several failed passes, a player from LSU caught the ball near the Auburn goal line right in front of where we sat. Everybody stood up as the Auburn and LSU players lined up against each other. Three times the football players on both sides dove into a big pile followed by a tremendous shout from the Auburn supporters. The clock showed twelve seconds remaining. “This is the game,” Dad said to no one in particular.

All the LSU players started right, chased by the Auburn players. Then one LSU player carrying the ball came running back to the left. Only one Auburn player stood between him and the goal line. The LSU player smashed into the Auburn man and together they fell into the end zone. The referee held two arms in the air for a touchdown. All the noise from the Auburn supporters instantly stopped. Across the stadium the LSU band played loudly as the purple-wearers celebrated.

Dad sat down and put his face in his hands. Mom put her arm around my shoulders and squeezed a little. Orange-wearers like us started quietly moving toward the exits. Dad stood up, sighed, and ruffled my hair a little. “Let’s show Jeremy some of the campus.”

* * *

Mom and Dad enjoyed the campus tour more than I did. They pointed out buildings and told stories about concerts, parties, football celebrations, old friends, and many odd-ball professors. As we walked around the sprawling campus, Mom complained about losing to LSU nearly every year, especially in Baton Rouge.

"Then why does Auburn play them?" I asked.

"Conference rules make us play all the other schools in our division," Dad explained. "But that isn't the only reason. We also play Georgia every year—when we don't have to—and lose more than we win. What makes life meaningful is trying to do the hard things."

"Even if you fail?"

"Especially if you might fail."

To me, that meant that Auburn was for losers. On the other hand, Mom and Dad loved Auburn and had enjoyed attending there. I felt glad that somebody had made a school for fossils like them.

I fell asleep in the car's backseat on the way back to Mobile. I woke briefly to hear Mom and Dad talking about the college fund they had started for me a few years earlier. *They've got my future all planned out,* I realized. *In just a few more years, I'll be able to create my own future.*

Chapter Ten

* * *

That fall and following winter America led the world into a major stock market crash and recession. Dad explained the crisis as caused by sub-prime loans sold to unqualified borrowers and bundling of mortgage-backed securities. Mom interpreted for me, "That means a lot of bankers got rich and normal people lost their homes."

Some of my classmates' parents lost homes or jobs. Dad's accounting firm lost some clients who went out of business. I heard Dad telling Mom that a lot of their retirement savings had been lost in the stock market. Some people predicted a depression like in the 1930s. In school, our history teacher showed us a video about the Great Depression—people out of work and standing in lines for food.

Dad, always conservative in financial issues, became even more cautious because of the uncertainty. Not me, though. I usually spent my piddling monthly allowance before mid-month. Mom and Dad had a firm rule, *No advances.* They maintained that trying to instill some money management principles even leading up to Christmas.

"Merry Christmas," I said as Mom opened her gift early December 25th.

Mom turned over the new phone, looking at it. "You got me a cell phone?"

"Sure, now you can call me even when you're not at home."

"Are you saying that you want more calls from me?"

"No, I didn't mean that. Just try it, Mom."

"You mean it's already active?"

"Sure, I bought a phone plan for you with Dad's gas card."

Dad had watched with interest. "Don't they give you the phone when you buy a plan?"

"Sort of," I confessed.

"Spent all your allowance money again, huh?"

"Pretty much."

"Do you remember that the credit card I loaned you is only for gas?"

"Sure. But I knew you'd want Mom to have a plan with her new phone."

Dad sighed and spoke to Mom, "Merry Christmas from me too, sweetheart."

Turned out that Mom loved her new phone. So much so, that for her birthday a couple of months later, I gave her my laptop. Of course, after that I needed a new and better laptop for school. Slowly I dragged my fossilized parents into the 2000s.

* * *

By age seventeen most of the guys at my church had stopped attending services and participating in youth group. But I had a reason to continue. Her name was Giselle.

In a month, Giselle would start eleventh grade, the same as me. She and a lot of kids from my church attended the private school, Mobile Academy.

Giselle was movie-star pretty, with a round face, pert nose, pouty lips, and wavy blond hair that rested on her shoulders. Her blue eyes seemed to twinkle. I admired everything about her, even the dark roots of her hair. She looked better than the Taylor Swift poster in my bedroom left over from my days as an immature kid. I just hoped Hollywood talent scouts wouldn't discover Giselle right away.

The previous year, Giselle, and most of the girls my age, had been taller than me. But since then I had started the growth spurt Mom had predicted. For those who don't know, growing pains are real. Your legs literally throb from aching. No matter. Once I had grown to her height, Giselle sometimes glanced at me during Bible study. Then she would look quickly away. I watched her a lot to see whether she noticed me.

That summer between my sophomore and junior years our youth pastor, Walter, organized a weekend youth retreat at a Christian camp. Mom and Dad dropped me off at the church. My heart soared when I saw Giselle among the girls. She glanced at me and sent a coy smile in my direction. The church's youth boarded a bus where I found the seat next to Giselle empty. She looked up at me and held her gaze. I dropped down beside her, my heart thumping.

For the first hour on the bus, Giselle and I bantered with those around us, ignoring one another. As the riders settled down, Giselle began to talk to me. "Like, I'm just glad to get away from home for a few days," she said. "My parents are so totally lame, you know. How are your parents?"

"Oh, yeah. I know what you mean," I sympathized. "My parents are from an old black-and-white movie. My mother even calls my father 'dinosaur.' Can you believe that?"

"I want to be so like your mother, though," offered Giselle.

"You mean really out-of-touch?"

"No, because everybody totally knows her. She's famous around Mobile."

As I started to pooh-pooh Mom's celebrity, Giselle continued, "My Dad is like a corporate lawyer. He only draws up contracts and licenses. He never goes to trial like lawyers on TV or anything. Nobody knows him."

"I've got you beat in the dull parent department. My father is an accountant." I thrilled that Giselle and I shared so much in common. Finally, Mom and Dad's retro values had come in handy.

Giselle grimaced. "That's major lameness, all right." She continued, "You know, I'm just counting the months until I can leave home for the University of Alabama. Where are you going to college?"

Suddenly the University of Alabama looked pretty good to me. "I'm thinking about going to Alabama, myself."

"That's awesome. What are you going to study?"

"Anything but accounting." As Giselle giggled, my mind raced for something, anything that sounded glamorous. "I'd like to be a surgeon, maybe." I started to insert, "Or an astronaut," but thought that could sound a little too ambitious, maybe like posturing.

"I'm, like, going to try out as a cheerleader at Alabama," Giselle countered. "That would open up a lot of doors for me. You know, help me to meet the right people."

Only a short step from there to Hollywood, I thought. I then raised her ante. "I'll probably study computer science at Alabama. Then I'll start an Internet company."

"OMG. That would be so rad for us to be there together. We could chill out and everything."

I wasn't sure what "everything" meant but rejoiced that it involved me. "What do you want to study at Alabama?"

"Does what I major in really matter? Oh, I don't mean to be an airhead or anything like that. It's just that being a lit major, or something, won't make me into somebody everybody knows."

Wow, I thought. *Giselle already knows who she wants to be. She wants to be somebody everybody knows. That's so cool.*

Two hours later the bus turned off the state highway and followed a winding gravel driveway to a retreat center. Unloading from the bus all of us saw a five-acre impounded lake, utilitarian lodge, chapel, dining hall, two dormitories, and a few cabins. Walter quickly designated one of the dorms for girls and the other for boys. "No boys in the girls' dorm and vice-versa."

Walter, with his Georgia wife and a couple of chaperones older than Mom and Dad, stayed in the cabins.

Inside the boys' dormitory, the other guys and I found a barracks-like line of single beds and a communal bathroom with shower. After dropping our backpacks, we reported to Walter at the lodge. I waited for Giselle to sit down then boldly took the seat beside her.

Walter soon had us singing songs and participating in skits. An hour or so later he gave an impassioned sermon about honoring God in your youth. That made sense to both Giselle and me. "You are the future of our faith," Walter exhorted us. "The future of Christianity is with you. And not the stale religion of the generations before us. But a new movement of young adults will reach the world for Jesus."

Giselle seemed entranced. I felt an excitement growing within myself. Giselle and I would together be part of God's reformation of Christianity.

The next morning, we had more music, Bible studies, and another rousing call to teenage devotion to God. Giselle and I prayed with the others to be mighty in God's power for Him.

After lunch, Walter gave his charges free time. Most of us headed for the lake. I'd seen girls in two-piece bathing suits. But this was the first time I ever really looked at a girl in a two-piece bathing suit. Giselle took my breath away. I wouldn't describe her as hot. That teenage term couldn't do justice to Giselle's womanly beauty. We spent the afternoon having water battles from floats and jumping off a platform onto an inflated raft that would bounce us high before we fell into the lake. Wet fun, Giselle in a bathing suit, and all somehow connected to Jesus.

After supper, another round of music and exhortation followed. Having directed his adolescent disciples in an upward direction, Walter, along with his wife and the elderly chaperones, retired to the cabins. That left us youth to entertain ourselves. Giselle and I found ourselves alone. I reached out to take her hand. Together we walked hand-in-hand on a barely lit path around the lake. She gushed over our futures. "You'll, like, be able to glorify God with your tech startup. And as an Alabama cheerleader I'll be an influence for Jesus. People will totally know who we are, you know." That night our futures, and indeed the future of the world in our hands, seemed secure.

Giselle gave me another coy smile. "You have your own car, don't you?"

"Of course," I answered as if I had bought it myself.

"That's totally awesome."

In a dark spot, we stopped. Giselle whispered, "Why don't you kiss me?"

That very thought had already occurred to me. I closed my eyes, leaned over, and gently put my lips on her chin. Giselle shifted her mouth to meet mine. Time stood still. We continued walking, occasionally stopping to kiss. I had learned to keep my eyes open until we connected. We hardly noticed the mosquitoes starting to descend on us. Eventually, Giselle slapped at one that had started to tap into her arm. Suddenly the mosquitoes seemed to form a cloud around us. We kissed one more time before fleeing into our respective dorms.

The following day was a blur. My mind rehearsed over and over the feel of Giselle's tender lips. I do remember we sat together at the youth worship service and on the bus going home. Occasionally our hands found each other's for a reassuring squeeze.

"Did you have a good time?" Mom asked when she picked me up at church.

"It was okay," I answered, still in a daze. But at last I realized what I wanted to be—Giselle's boyfriend and eventually her husband.

Chapter Eleven

* * *

Fall semester of my junior year brought fresh opportunities. West Side High School's traveling tennis team only accommodated twelve players. Well, that's how many players the school's van held. So, effectively, the top twelve became the team. The rest of us aspiring tennis hopefuls just practiced among ourselves.

Graduation of the seniors the previous spring had opened some coveted van seats. Through the tenth grade, I'd never managed to rank higher than seventeenth among those hoping for a van seat. A new ranking would determine my fate. To establish ranking, our tennis coach arranged a double-elimination tournament seeded by the previous year's ranking. Without the previous year's seniors, my seeding rose to eleventh among fourteen seeds. But six underclassmen coming up from the ninth grade would also be eligible. Figuring that making the traveling tennis team would surely impress Giselle, I resolved to win a seat.

I lost the first round 6-2, 6-1 to a six-foot-tall state-ranked former ninth grader. He had a wicked topspin to complement a serve and volley game. In the losers' bracket, I won against another rising ninth grader. I then managed to beat the thirteenth seed, a classmate of mine. By then the higher seeded players had started falling into the one-loss bracket. I lost 6-2, 6-4 to the fourth seed, a senior, and finished the tournament ranked fourteenth.

Mom had attended and stoically watched all my matches. "There's always next year," she encouraged after I had retreated to the safety of home to sulk.

"I'm quitting tennis," I reported.

"You don't have to give up."

"I'll never make the top twelve." And my tennis career thereby ended after five years.

* * *

I picked up the ringing phone upstairs. "Hello."

"Could I speak with Katie Parker?" I recognized the high-pitched nasal voice of Mrs. Hamsby, our school guidance counselor. Just the week before, she and I had completed my required career opportunities review.

"Mom!" I called. "There's someone on the phone for you." Once I heard Mom answer, I hit the phone mouthpiece against the base as if hanging up but didn't disconnect.

Eavesdropping, I heard, "Katie, this is Sandra Hamsby at West Side High. Our policy is to inform our parents of any career advice dispensed."

"Thank you for calling," Mom said.

"Your son, Jeremy, is a nice boy. Likable. Respectful. Cooperative. Smart. He seems to have self-confidence. During our career opportunities review, Jeremy said something about being a medical surgeon or starting an Internet company. But you know his grades are not outstanding. I told Jeremy he had to start applying himself if he wants to reach those dreams."

Mom sighed. "You're right. His father and I have prodded him occasionally. I taught teenagers for eleven years myself. I know that if you push kids too hard, they can dig in their heels. Jeremy has those stubborn tendencies. Unfortunately, a couple of years ago his father and I got our priorities mixed up and neglected him. Since then we may have been overly lenient. Maybe Jeremy doesn't feel the urgency to try hard. As you know, every parent wants their child to excel. No matter how much we love our son and how special he is to us, in academics Jeremy is just an ordinary kid."

My mind reeled. Just an ordinary kid?

Sympathy tinged Mrs. Hamsby's voice. "I know what you mean. My own son went through some difficult phases. Sometimes you just want to force these kids into realizing their potential before they waste their chances."

"His father and I see great potential in Jeremy," Mom insisted.

"We all do." Mrs. Hamsby continued, "The kids working toward college placement are taking the entrance exams this fall. Jeremy didn't take the practice exams last year. Is he preparing for the actual exams?"

I heard Mom sigh again and answer evasively. "He has the prep books."

"Well, anything you can do to get him focused could make a big difference."

"Okay," Mom responded. "Thanks again for calling."

I waited for Mom to hang up before putting the receiver down. In my room, I found the stack of preparatory study books for the ACT and SAT exams Mom had purchased. She'd hinted that I might find them useful. I flipped through some of the uninteresting topics. Sitting down to the tedious business of learning what ten years of school hadn't taught me seemed a worse fate than death.

The memory of Giselle and our time together a few weeks earlier at the lake intruded into my thoughts. Since then, I'd seen her a few times in the youth group at church. She had disguised our relationship by pretending to not notice me, by acting distant. But we hadn't had the opportunity to be alone again. I thought that maybe I could ask her to a movie.

Then I hesitated. Giselle had recently been elected to the fifteen-girl cheerleading squad at her private high school. That proved her to be popular. Maybe I should burnish my own popularity status before risking a movie invitation.

What does being popular take? I asked myself. Athletic ability certainly helped. Brody had finally entered tenth grade and had instantly become our school's starting quarterback. Even though he was an underclassman to most of West Side's students, nobody could match his popularity. My tennis career was a washout—no help for me would come in athletics.

Few, if any, of the most popular kids showed much interest in studies. I did have lack of scholarly inclination going for me. Looks could also be a major factor. Mom—reinforced by Grandmother—had always called me "handsome." I looked in the mirror to see a baby-faced boy five feet seven inches tall and just over 115 pounds. Cute to a mother and grandmother, maybe. A few red pimples further marred my alleged handsomeness.

Although my school had prohibited beards, a lot of the most popular guys in the junior and senior classes, plus sophomore Brody, sported a not-shaven look. Nothing improved a guy's status so much as being sent home to shave. I had just a little fuzz on my chin at that point and looked forward to needing a cut. I decided to start shaving regularly anyway, if for no other reason than to hide the sparsity of my facial growth. I tallied only one out of three of the popularity factors.

I knew there must be other paths to popularity. I resolved to find them. Returning to the test preparation books never occurred to me. I couldn't jeopardize my future with Giselle by being labeled "a brain." To placate Mom and Dad, I did take the college entrance tests during fall of my junior year. Miserable scores came back. Mom and Dad gave each other baleful looks.

* * *

One other factor would perhaps translate into popularity—a car. Albeit decrepit, the high-mileage Toyota qualified as a ride. I started my popularity campaign by making myself available to give lifts to classmates, especially the more popular ones. That way I'd be seen with the in group. That appeared to be working because soon I had a lot of riders. Not Brody, of course. His parents had given him a new Mustang for being named to the pre-season all-conference football team.

My observations soon told me that some of the popular guys acted like renegades. They asserted their maturity by breaking as many rules as possible. I started hanging out with some of those who aspired to be bad boys. *Being good is for kids,* I told myself. I didn't exactly shun any of my previous friends, the non-popular ones. Neither did I attempt to spend any time with them.

"Come on, Jeremy," one of my newer companions urged. "Drive us to Jonesy's house. He just got the new Xbox 360 and his parents are at work. You can be back before anyone misses you."

"I've got a class."

"You call PE a class? Who's going to miss you?"

Probably nobody, I admitted to myself.

"You know that Coach McCracken never calls roll. No one will tell him."

Chapter Twelve

* * *

"Okay. Just to Jonesy's house then. I'll drop you off there," I offered. But on our way to Jonesy's house, the guys insisted we stop at a convenience store. Inside I watched them try to use a fake ID to buy beer. They tried three places with no luck. By then, PE hour had ended.

"You're better off not trying to sneak in now," one of my riders suggested.

I never got back to school that day. My cell phone rang during last period. "Where are you, Jeremy?" Principal Snyder asked. Apparently, Coach McCracken didn't call roll often, but he could count. When the number of teenage guys lining up for calisthenics looked low, he asked the group, "Who's missing?" After everybody shrugged, out came the roll book.

* * *

Mom didn't say anything to me when I got home after serving the first of five consecutive detentions for skipping class. She waited for Dad to get home, something she had never done before.

Supper seemed normal until Dad asked me how my day went.

"Not bad. I got a B on my geometry test." I thought maybe the good grade would divert their attention.

"Your Mom said that you came home late. Did you have some after-school activity you didn't tell us about?"

"Just a little extra work. Nothing important."

Mom couldn't restrain herself any longer. "You're digging yourself in deeper and deeper."

Then I realized that they knew what I had done. I never did have a good face for hiding guilt. "Listen, I made a mistake. It won't happen again."

"Why did you cut classes?" Dad persisted.

"I was taking some guys somewhere."

Mom stared at me as if I had held up a liquor store. "Where?"

"To Jonesy's house."

"Is that all?" Dad asked.

"Yeah."

Dad shook his head. "Then why did it take so long?"

"It just did."

"Jeremy, one of my clients called. He said that four underage teenagers including you came into his store trying to buy beer."

"All I did was drive the guys."

"And you would have been the one arrested and put in jail for drinking and driving."

I grasped that silence was my best, my only, defense.

Mom came back into the interrogation. "Do you have anything else to say?"

By then I knew better than to say anything more that might incriminate me further. She continued by speaking to Dad. "I'm thinking a week without driving the car."

"And add on another week for not being up-front with us," he replied. "And after that, he'll drive no place but to school and back for a month."

"Good idea," Mom agreed. "No cell phone either. I won't need to call him anyway."

So that derailed my thoughts about taking Giselle to a movie.

The worst part about my grounding was that Mom had to pick me up at school again. That didn't help my standing among my rebellious would-be peers at all.

My class-cutting escapade with the renegades did win me a little notoriety. Being a "bad boy" had even gotten me the attention of some members of the opposite sex. One afternoon I heard some of the more popular girls talking about me in the school library. The girls couldn't see me because of a stack of books between us.

"Jeremy *is* cute," one girl said.

I leaned in to hear more. "But he's such a mama's boy," a different voice countered. Listening in horror, I heard other descriptive words. "Immature. Childish. Hangs out with losers."

The girls walked my way laughing among themselves. I ran to avoid being seen, carrying my shame with me. So, my lack of popularity came down to Mom and Dad's fault. I would have to find ways to distance myself from my parents. Them and the Parker legacy.

* * *

My first step involved ignoring Mom and Dad in public. Once I finished my punishment, they had let me use the phone and car again. Technically I still answered Mom's calls. To do otherwise would cost me mobility–the car–and cut off my communications–the cell phone. But I let Mom's calls ring a long time before answering. I figured that would prove my independence to anybody nearby who might hear.

Next, I carefully examined my parents' values, purposing to do the opposite. Punctuality, respectfulness, frugality, neatness, patience, politeness, thoughtfulness, generosity–all discarded. I hadn't seen Giselle at church youth group recently, so I stopped attending myself. I simply tried to do everything the opposite of Mom and Dad.

Mom noticed my change of demeanor and tried talking. "Jeremy, you seem a little distracted lately. Are you doing all right? Any problems at school?"

Dad tried reasoning with me. "Son, you've got great potential. You can do wonderful things with your life, if you'll start concentrating."

But talking seriously to Mom and Dad could be the worst mistake possible. Knowing how I felt might lead them to interfere. Or maybe they would try to reinforce some of their outdated ideas. In truth, I didn't like the new Jeremy very much. But I would do whatever necessary to find a new path for myself.

* * *

Despite my efforts at rebellion, my strategy to gain respect among potential friends bore little fruit. No invitations to parties. No girls looking my way. No snappy nickname. I remembered Dad mentioning many times how popular Mom had been in college. And after her campaigns to help the school system, nearly everybody in Mobile liked and admired her. In desperation, I risked asking Mom what popularity required.

After overcoming her surprise at being consulted on such a personal issue, she assured me, "You have lots of friends, honey."

I couldn't face the humiliation of telling Mom what I'd heard the girls saying about me, especially the part about being a mama's boy. I gave a guarded explanation. "But my friends aren't popular themselves. Who you hang out with . . ." I trailed off, leaving the conclusion unsaid.

"Jeremy, popularity in high school isn't all you think it is. A lot of kids who are considered popular aren't very nice people. High school can be a cruel environment. I taught teenagers for a lot of years, remember?"

I *had* forgotten that. A logical side of me had to acknowledge that maybe Mom could have some valid insights. "Well, what should I do?"

She started with the old cliché, "If you like people, they'll like you."

I tried not to show impatience. "Okay, but something more concrete than that."

Mom thought a minute. "Why don't you try inviting some of the popular kids to go fishing with you and your father?"

Genius! My Mom was a genius. "Do you think Dad would?"

"Your father will do anything for you, honey."

"Thanks, Mom." I started to leave armed with her great idea.

"Jeremy, could I tell you one more thing?"

Obligation required me to listen. "Okay."

"Once you start college, high school popularity won't mean anything. Zilch. Your father and I are concerned about you getting into a good school. A school where your natural talents can mature and flourish. Can you try a little harder with your studies? You can prepare and retake the entrance exams your senior year."

"Sure, Mom." *And blow the one popularity factor I have going for me?* I said to myself.

* * *

Dad did take out three guys I invited to go deep-sea fishing during Christmas break. Since they were underage, he wouldn't let them bring beer on the boat. They overlooked that fossilized decree when lots of fish started coming in. Dad orchestrated the entire day to make me look good. I piloted the boat, showed the guys how to fish, and tried to look modest when Dad told them how I'd helped him catch the sailfish. After taking pictures of the group with our catch, Dad expertly cleaned their fish. Aside from the lack of beer, the day could not have gone better for the guys.

And Mom's idea worked. Well enough, anyway, to get me an invitation to a Mardi Gras party at a big estate on the west coast of Mobile Bay. Some guy's parents had gone to their own weekend-long party, leaving their son home alone. I drove myself to the party in the decrepit Toyota. I found the long driveway lined with newer, expensive cars. More cars parked on the lawn. I recognized Brody's Mustang among them. He remained the most popular guy at West Side High. As a seventeen-year-old sophomore, Brody had led our school to the state championship game and had been named as all-state in football. Universities with major football programs had already started recruiting him.

Loud music could be heard a block away. A lot of high-school athletes, college students, and some high-school graduates in their twenties jammed the house and a large patio in the backyard. I immediately noticed how provocatively the girls dressed. I heard a whole new vocabulary of foul language.

Everybody drank beer and most of them smoked. A few carried bottles of whisky. I had thought athletes didn't drink or smoke. Apparently, Mardi Gras suspended that rule. Somebody put a can of beer in my hand. Dad sometimes drank beer with clients, but never at home. Only on rare special occasions did Mom and Dad drink a glass of wine. I sipped the beer. My first reaction was to spit it out, but I knew better in front of the people I wanted to impress.

I stayed on the patio for the relatively smoke-free air. I kept drinking beer, laughing at the jokes the others told, and trying to look like I fit in. That eventually became boring. I drifted into the house where the party got rowdier. There I found Giselle sitting on a couch with a drink in one hand and a cigarette in the other. Our eyes met. She looked away without acknowledging me. As I watched, a guy with a dark stubble of whiskers pulled her up from the couch, grabbed her bottom, and then led her away by the hand. The guy was Brody Nelson.

Nobody noticed me slipping away from the party. I could hardly think through the confusion in my head. *Is partying like that what popularity requires? If so, then you really are a dweeb. You were trying to be popular to impress Giselle. You'll never be able to compete with Brody.*

Knowing that I'd drunk alcohol, I drove slowly and carefully toward home. So slowly that I blocked traffic. A police patrol car fell in behind me. My heart sank when the flashing blue lights came on. After I pulled over, a tall middle-aged patrolman approached the driver's side window and asked for my license and vehicle registration. His nametag read "Vance." As he looked at my driver's license with a flashlight, he asked, "Are you Katie Parker's son?"

"Yes, sir."

"Where are you going?"

"I'm headed home."

"Have you been drinking, Mr. Parker?"

I remembered how evading the truth had gotten me into deeper trouble after skipping class. "Just a little beer, sir."

The officer reached to his belt and pulled off a device. "Blow into this."

After I did, he looked at the device and said, "You're slightly over the legal limit for alcohol, son." I sat frozen in fear and dismay. The officer paused to consider the situation.

"Do you have any open containers with alcohol in the car?"

"No, sir."

"Your mother, Mrs. Parker, has done a lot for our schools. Here's what I want you to do. I'm going to turn off the flashing lights and pull the squad car in front of you. I want you to follow me to your house. You live on Sycamore Street, right? That's only a mile from here. And Mr. Parker, understand that if I ever catch you driving over the legal limit for alcohol again, you're going to jail no matter how close to home you are."

I nearly fainted from relief. "Yes, I live on Sycamore Street. Thank you, Officer Vance."

The officer led me by our house and paused to make sure I turned into the driveway. Mom and Dad had already gone to bed. I took off my clothes reeking of tobacco and alcohol and put them in the washer. Learning how to wash clothes at the Hobbses' had paid off. Then I brushed my teeth and went to bed. *I'll figure it all out tomorrow,* I told myself.

Chapter Thirteen

* * *

But the following morning, I hardly knew what to think. What had happened to Giselle? Just a few months ago we had planned to influence the world together. She had changed. Or had she? Could some people simply fit into whatever environment they found themselves? And honesty required me to recognize that Giselle's life goal had been to be somebody everybody knew. Being with Brody would be a logical opportunity for her.

I figured that some people, Mom and Dad for instance, didn't let the environment change them. But wait! Mom and Dad had changed when they wanted to—after I tried to run away. They bought the boat and became more fun. That wasn't the same as changing to act like the people around them, though, like Giselle.

And what about me? The one nearly arrested for drinking and driving? Should I become like the popular people I'd seen at the party? Is that what would be required to gain the interest of a pretty girl? The old adult cliché "Just be yourself" came back to me. Did I know the myself I should be? Who did I want to be?

Everything overwhelmed my ability to think. Unsure of what to do, in the next few months I retreated from a lot of social interactions. I gave up on Giselle; in fact, I gave up on girls in general at least for the time being. I just didn't know how to act around them. I went back to my previous school friends, those of the twerpy, unpopular type. Ruthie would always be my faithful, consistent friend. And going out on the boat with Mom and Dad, despite their maddeningly old-fashioned ways, never got old. On the boat, I had a best friend in Dad.

Although I still didn't have any idea what to do with my life, I didn't want to completely write off the possibility of college. Over the summer break prior to my senior year, I reluctantly applied myself to preparing for the college entrance exams, albeit without much enthusiasm. I sort of felt like I'd be doing Mom and Dad a favor by investing a little effort. Mom and Dad gratefully tutored me. Mom wasn't a bad science teacher, not as good in English. Dad handled math and history. He knew the subjects but couldn't communicate them as well as Mom did hers. The three of us had several arguments about my lack of concentration.

But both Mom and Dad also deliberately tried to make that summer fun. Since I would graduate from high school before the following summer, I'm certain they wanted to make my last summer holiday with them enjoyable. On a two-week trip, we all went to Disney World and Universal Studios in Orlando. Then we camped at Key Largo to snorkel on the coral reefs and drove all the way to Key West.

Shorter trips that summer included Atlanta and Braves baseball, museums and a zoo in Birmingham, the Grand Old Opry in Nashville, and a visit to The Hermitage—Andrew Jackson's plantation. From Nashville, we drove the entire length of the Natchez Trace Parkway that Daniel Parker had traveled to fight the British at New Orleans. We took a ride on a Mississippi River boat. All these trips felt like being on the Audit together, except without Ruthie. We also did lots of fishing and boating on Mobile Bay and the gulf. Ruthie always came with us on the boat.

I started to see that Mom and Dad's lives really weren't so bad, thanks to having me to entertain . . . but I still didn't think I wanted to grow up to be like them.

In the fall, I retook both the ACT and SAT tests and scored much better than the previous year. Not good enough scores for Auburn or Alabama. But probably good enough to get into some college. Mom and Dad visibly appeared relieved.

Those tests completed, I let my schoolwork lapse again. Maybe I took science for granted since that had been my best result on the SAT. The result: I completely forgot about the science project required of all seniors. "Forgot" would be a kind exaggeration. I put off thinking about the project until the day before it came due. There would be no graduation without some sort of project. Although even a D minus project would let me graduate, I had nothing.

Where was the first place to go in any crisis? Mom. I must have caught her on a bad day. She stood stunned when I asked her what to do about my next-day-due science project. She shook her head in disbelief and exasperation before saying, "Why don't you do a scientific survey study on the reasons parents want to kill their teenagers? Your father will have a lot to add when he gets home." Then Mom walked away, leaving me to my fate.

I marveled that for the only time ever, Mom had abandoned me. But I had no other idea than hers to try. In my bedroom, I created a crude survey for parents to evaluate their teenagers and their occasional desire to murder them. I included choices like irresponsible, lazy, disobedient, disrespectful, stupid, sloppy, ugly, argumentative, expensive, dishonest, and too time-consuming.

I got on the phone and made thirty-one calls that night. I called until parents started telling me, "We've gone to bed, dammit." Not only did I tally their responses, but after promising confidentiality, I recorded a lot of witty and sarcastic things the parents said, like, "Parenting teens involves lots of anger, eye rolling, and wanting to run away—and that's just the parents!" I stayed up all night organizing and typing my results including a lot of the extra comments. I drew conclusions and added a few first-person examples from my own life with Mom and Dad. I used the story about insisting on the expensive athletic shoes, then Zeek eating one. Despite myself, I enjoyed doing that science project.

The next morning, I turned in the project on time and hoped for that D minus. I anticipated the worst when I heard some teachers talking and laughing over my submission. I looked with trepidation when our science teacher posted the project grades. I could hardly believe my eyes—A+. All my friends, and some others I didn't know well, slapped me on the back and congratulated me. Somebody—probably my science teacher, who was a parent himself—Xeroxed my paper and distributed it. The school newspaper printed excerpts of my work for the entire student body to read.

At home, I expected Mom and Dad to rejoice when I brought home a rare high score. They just sat blank-faced, looking at me. Not knowing how to react to their indifference, I left the graded project with them. Pausing at my usual place out of sight at the top of the stairs, I waited. Soon I heard chuckling. Finally, Dad said, "That kid could be a genius, if only he'd apply himself."

Ah, I thought, *Dad finally recognizes my talent.*

Mom answered him, "That's true of ninety percent of teenaged boys. Jeremy's just an ordinary kid in that regard."

Still an ordinary kid? I wondered, *How can I make myself more than ordinary?* One successful project wasn't enough.

The science project episode did make me a bit of a celebrity at school. I discovered that I had a talent for spoofing parents and adults in general. I realized, *Now I've got a way to distinguish myself.* I felt a resurgence of desire to be popular. Sassing teachers broadened my appeal among my classmates. One time I was talking in class and missed what our economics and government teacher, Mr. Pritchard, had said. In a stern voice he asked me, "Jeremy, do I need to repeat myself?"

I responded, "No, sir. I ignored you just fine the first time."

Chapter Fourteen

* * *

Driving away from school an hour later, I figured that my two-day suspension would skyrocket my popularity among my classmates. They would consider me a martyr for overworked students. Of course, the teacher grapevine informed Mom within hours about my disrespectful sarcasm. She grounded me for two weeks without any phone or car privileges. That lasted only until Dad heard. He extended my penalty to a month. Being cut off from all the other kids didn't help my popularity at all.

* * *

After the Christmas holidays, I still hadn't applied to any colleges. Almost daily Mom or Dad would ask about my progress. Some exciting advertisements on TV caught my attention. They showed handsome men and women jumping out of airplanes, heroically rescuing people, and seeing the world.

The next afternoon I stopped by the armed services recruiting office in a local strip mall. There army, navy, and air force representatives nearly fell over each other jostling to talk with me. Never had anyone expressed such eagerness to have Jeremy Parker. Certainly, no girls, sports teams, or colleges had. The recruiters offered a plethora of exciting choices and even a signing bonus large enough to buy a brand-new car of my own. Although the Iraq and Afghanistan wars had de-escalated in 2010, the army sergeant, with tattoos on his arms and wearing a Purple Heart medal, assured me that plenty of action remained.

With my eighteenth birthday just a few weeks away, the recruiters offered to sign me up immediately. If I felt necessary, they would even visit my parents to reassure them and thank them for providing such a fine young man to their nation's service. I couldn't decide between the different armed services and took home an armful of colorful literature. All the brochures showed pretty women in uniform one would presumably meet on duty. Mom, to whom my bedroom had never been off limits, found the literature nearly immediately. The next night I heard tapping on my door. Then Dad stuck his head in. "Can I come in?" he politely asked.

I looked up from admiring a picture of a group of attractive men and women in fatigues exploring an exotic open-air market somewhere in the Middle East. "Sure, Dad."

He gestured toward the literature. "Mind if I look at some of those?"

"Help yourself."

After leafing through several brochures, I heard him clear his throat and readied myself to defend my yet un-made decision.

"Your mother and I don't mind, if you want to join the military," he started. "Well, your mother does, but she'll support your decision," he corrected himself. "We Parkers have always been pretty patriotic."

That sounded positive. I said, "A Parker in every war. We wouldn't want to break that tradition."

Dad forced a smile. "That's true. But the ones I knew personally regretted the necessity of that. My grandfather came home from World War I partially deaf from an exploding shell. My father fought in France during the Second World War. He would never talk about any part of that. But your grandmother told me that the war had made him harder. She said my father rarely laughed after the war like he did before. And I think your mother told you about your uncle Chuck."

"He committed suicide, didn't he?"

"Yes, he did. Chuck became addicted to drugs and shot himself in the head. And that resulted directly from the Vietnam war. He had to do things there that haunted him until he couldn't stand living anymore." I remained silent. Dad waited several long minutes before continuing, "You can join the military. And if our country is threatened enough to implement a draft, I'll urge you to join. But your mother and I ask you to consider postponing enlisting for a few years. You can explore other options life offers first, especially college. Going to college can be about a lot more than learning the content of books. I started college like a person outlined in a coloring book. I left college colored in with values and abilities. If you're serious about military life, you could take ROTC in college. Then, if you joined afterwards, you'd be an officer with more opportunities."

I remained silent again. Dad rose to go. "Well, thanks for hearing me out, Son."

As he left, I said, "Thanks, Dad. Tell Mom I won't do anything right away. Without talking it over with you both."

Dad nodded tight-lipped in gratitude and slipped out.

I didn't enlist, but simply dithered making any decision about my future. And that brings me to the springtime when I met Tara–the answer to all my indecision–the path to an undreamed-about future.

Chapter Fifteen

* * *

The day after meeting Tara at the sports park I continued to imagine her parting words—"See you later, cutie"—as an invitation to return. But I told myself that she had nothing to do with my skipping Sunday church and heading back to the park. My heart leaped a little at seeing her sitting on the same bench with her long legs crossed. For a while, I watched from a distance from behind a bleacher overlooking a softball diamond. Summoning my courage, I started strolling toward her, trying to look casual. If Tara noticed, she made no sign. I walked past her without speaking and felt like the world's biggest loser. Then from behind me I heard, "Well hello, Jeremy Parker. Find that girlfriend yet?"

Turning, I saw her wry smile, the same green eyes, her long-braided hair, tanned skin, and the same attitude of nonchalance. I tried to act surprised with well-rehearsed words. "Oh, hi. You're still here. How's business?" Unfortunately, my voice wavered a bit.

"Business stinks! I'm thinking of lowering my price to a dollar. Maybe then I could collect enough for supper." Her deep husky voice contrasted with the high-pitched lilt of southern girls. The sexiness of that made my knees feel loose. Not much about her appearance or demeanor resembled anything feminine in my world.

"What type of food do you like?" was the only thing I could think of to say.

"What I like is steak and lobster. But I'll probably have to settle for hot-water noodles from a package."

On an impulse I blurted out, "How about I take you to lunch?"

Tara looked me up and down while maintaining that smile. "Why not? Nothing much going on here."

I pointed toward a burger restaurant across the street from the park. "Does that place look okay?"

By way of answer, she picked up her fortune-telling sign. "Lead the way, cutie."

* * *

Inside the restaurant, Tara ordered a loaded bacon cheeseburger with fried onion rings and a large chocolate shake. I got the same. As Tara ate, she occasionally licked her fingers. Somehow, she made the unrefined gesture seem sophisticated, even alluring.

"How did you learn to read palms?" I asked.

"I majored in fortune-telling at Yale."

"You can study fortune-telling at college?"

"No, silly boy. I majored in theater at a liberal arts college." She named a school I'd never heard of, probably because they didn't sponsor Division I sports. Between bites, Tara continued explaining, "After three years at college, I split because the whole scene became a downer. Although I liked playing a role, I just didn't have the burning desire to have people watching me that's needed to succeed in theater. And all the males at college just wanted to drink, act like big shots, and try getting me into bed."

"What did you do after leaving college?"

"When your plans don't work out, you suck it up and go. I decided to hike the Appalachian trail. Most people try south to north. But I started in Maine and headed for Georgia. I met a fella named Bennie traveling the same direction as me. Every night we wound up at the same shelter. But we had started too late in the year to finish. Snows caught us in West Virginia and drove us off the trail."

Tara looked wistful, as if regretting the necessity of quitting her journey. "Then Bennie suggested we pool what little money each of us had to buy a used van. I didn't understand at the time why he wanted to register our van only in my name. He later ran a red light in Texas and got arrested on an outstanding warrant for jumping bail. The warrant accused him of possession of marijuana with intent to distribute. That charge had to be bogus. Bennie would never have parted with any weed. The local police extradited him to New Hampshire where they locked him up with no chance of parole for at least five years. I kept the van to travel and live in."

"You lived in a van?"

"Oh, yeah. I still do. After hiking eight hundred miles on a wilderness trail, the van seems like a luxury penthouse. All you need is your camping gear and a place to park. When you want a hot shower, you can get a spot in a campground for fifteen dollars or go to some truck stops. But I like the parking lots of all-night stores like Walmart. There you can park, use a restroom, get food and cheap gas without paying a camp fee. The van took Bennie and me to hike in colorful fall leaves in New England and to trails in the Rocky Mountains. Once at an interstate rest area in Iowa, a blizzard snowed us into the van. We spent four days drinking herbal tea and just hanging loose. We took off all our clothes and lay side by side with everything we had piled on top of us to stay warm. How many people can say they've had that opportunity?"

"Not many," I acknowledged and picked up the check the waitress had left. Twenty-three dollars exceeded my expectation. I didn't have that much cash. Fortunately, I did have the credit card Dad had given me for gas. Prodded by the necessity of paying the bill, I asked, "Where do you get money on the road?"

"Well, I'm finding out that palm reading is no good. But there are lots of other ways. Sometimes Bennie and I raided fountains in the night. He had this little scoop that would scrape the coins right off the bottom. Or you can usually find a few coins around the drive-through of fast food restaurants or under vending machines. People drop them and don't pick them up. When you need money fast, you can approach people in parking lots or gas stations, tell a sad story, and ask them for food or gas. Most are in a hurry and give you cash. But a few actually buy you food. In a day, we usually could fill up our tank with gas and the van with potato chips and lunch meat plus rake in a hundred dollars or more. Once I tried standing at an intersection with a sign that said 'Will work for food.' A police car stopped, and the officer told me to move on. I was mad until I realized what he had thought. Letting anybody use me is one way I won't get money."

The waitress came back and pointed at the check. "I can take this, if y'all are finished." I took that as a hint to vacate the table, paid the bill with Dad's credit card, added a tip, and led Tara to the door. But I wanted to stay with her, look at her, and hear her voice. "Where are you from?" I asked as we walked back toward the park.

"My parents are genuine long-haired hippies from the sixties and seventies. They lived on a communal farm in Wisconsin. That's where I was born. Now they work at a dry cleaner in Madison, get stoned, and watch TV all night. I wanted more from life than my parents experienced. I'll bet you want more than your parents, too."

I nodded vigorously in agreement. "Yeah, I want more from life than them. My parents are so old-fashioned that they skipped the sixties and seventies. They should be shown in a museum as fossils."

Nodding herself, Tara continued, "I do believe in saving the planet, like my parents. But I want to be *in* the environment, not just talk about saving it. That's why I came down south last winter. Easier to be outside without a blizzard going on."

Tara sat back on the bench where she had started and patted next to her for me to sit down. Once I sat, she turned to me. "Now what about you, Jeremy Parker? You're more than eighteen, right?"

"Oh sure, I'm over eighteen." In my head I said, *By three months.* Then I tried to be funny. "Are you over eighteen?"

She laughed a little and hit my arm lightly with her fingers. "You're sweet. I'm twenty-three. But tell me something about yourself."

So I described my life to her, trying to make it sound exciting. Although Tara listened attentively, my descriptions of fishing with my father and playing volleyball on the beach sounded pathetic in my own ears. To get away from my own recital of the mundane, I asked, "Is your van near here? Can I see it?"

Tara stood up. "Why not? It's just a couple of blocks from here."

She led me to a shopping center parking lot. There sat a late-model van with a windowless sliding door. "Home sweet home," she said as she unlocked and slid open the door.

Inside lay an air mattress and a crumpled sleeping bag. In one corner, a portable propane stove–the kind backpackers use–sat with an aluminum pot. Another corner had a heap of unfolded clothes. Camping gear filled the passenger seat. A pile of outdoors-oriented paperback books and novels plus some music CDs lay to one side along with an older laptop. A rechargeable LED lantern was plugged into the van's lighter. To me, the entire setup looked like a magic carpet ride to a life of adventure.

I realized while I'd been admiring Tara's home, she had been describing her circumstances of being marooned in Mobile.

". . . Then the engine started overheating. The garage needs $500 to install a salvage-yard radiator. Without the new radiator I can only get about sixty miles on a water fill up. Even then I'm risking ruining the engine. That means I'm stuck here until I can find the money."

"Can't you get money by asking people for food, like you described?"

Tara shook her head. "That's risky to try in an area where you're staying. The police might arrest you for running a scam. You never want to get arrested. Bad things can happen in any jail."

Suddenly I remembered that I had promised Dad to help him carry in and install a new dishwasher he had bought to replace Mom's old one. I looked at my cell phone. Late already. "I've got to go, Tara. Can I have your cell phone number?"

"I don't have a cell phone. But here's my email address. I check email occasionally by parking near a Starbucks and using their Wi-Fi."

"I've taken up your entire afternoon. No chance for you to earn supper money now." I gave her a ten-dollar bill—nearly my last money—to buy supper.

She took the bill and gave me her wonderful smile. "Thanks for lunch and dinner. Will I see you tomorrow, cutie?"

"Maybe. I've got something to do until later in the afternoon." I didn't tell her the something was finishing my last weeks of high school.

"I like you, Jeremy. I hope you do come back." Tara then stood on her toes to kiss me on the cheek.

I hurried away with my cheek burning and my heart thumping. *She's beautiful. She really likes me. A girl who appreciates me. A girl who needs my help.* The thought of our imminent prom also reoccurred to me.

Chapter Sixteen

* * *

Late Monday afternoon after school I returned to the sports park for the third straight day. This time I congratulated myself for walking directly up to Tara. I tried to convey confidence and just a touch of intimacy. "Business any better today?"

Tara had seen me coming and resumed her wry smile. "Feels better now that you're here."

She's glad to see you! my libido shouted within me.

I had withdrawn some money from an ATM with Dad's credit card and pin number. "How about supper with me tonight?"

"Lead the way, Jeremy Parker."

After sharing two large loaded pizzas, I steered Tara toward a walk around the park in the twilight. "Have you made any progress collecting money for the radiator?" I asked. To myself I hoped, *Please say no.*

To my relief Tara answered, "No." Then she matter-of-factly added, "But tomorrow will be better. I'm going to rob a bank."

I must have looked startled, because she corrected herself. "I'm just kidding about the bank. I'll probably just knock off a couple of convenience stores."

I stopped walking. "Don't do it, Tara!"

My concern seemed to amuse her. "Well, okay, if you say not, Jeremy Parker." She shrugged in exaggerated regret. "And I don't have a gun anyway."

Her smile told me that I'd been fooled again. I resumed walking in a bit of a huff. Sensing my pique, Tara reassured me, "I don't want to do anything that could get me arrested, silly boy. Being locked up would be so terrible. Just being stuck inside a town is about to drive me crazy." She waved at her surroundings. "I'm hanging loose around this crappy park to sort of be outdoors."

"I could take you to some outdoors places."

"Like where?"

"Some parks across the bay."

Tara turned to look at me. Her face looked odd without the whimsical smile. "You could? Right now?"

I knew that Mom and Dad would be expecting me to be home soon. I dreaded a cellphone call from Mom with Tara listening. "No, I can't right now. How about I pick you up here next Saturday morning?"

"Sure. Why not? I'm not going anywhere."

My heart soared. I had made a date with a beautiful, vivacious woman. "Okay, then. I'll meet you here at nine. Here's what I have to help you this week." I gave Tara all the money I had remaining from the ATM withdrawal–nineteen dollars.

She took the money. "Thanks! I do have one question, though."

I expected she would need some assurances for her safety before going to an unknown place with someone she had only met in the park. "What's that?"

"When is Saturday? I don't know the day of the week."

* * *

On Saturday morning I could hardly wait to meet Tara and arrived at our park bench by eight a.m. To my surprise, I found her already sitting on the bench waiting. She wore the same clothes I had seen her wearing every day. I was even more surprised to see a policeman talking to her. Uncharacteristically, Tara kept her head down and appeared nervous. Officer Vance, the same officer who had caught me driving just over the legal alcohol limit and then taken me home, turned as I approached.

"Good morning, Mr. Parker. Do you know this woman?"

"Yes, sir. This is Tara." I then realized that I didn't know her last name.

"And how do know Ms. Tara?"

"She's my friend. We're going to the east shore today."

Officer Vance looked back and forth between us then stared with suspicion at Tara. "We've had some reports of a con person soliciting money with artful tales of woe in this area. That's a misdemeanor in Mobile, subject to arrest."

"Thank you, officer Vance. I'll vouch for Tara."

Officer Vance looked at me again. "Okay, Mr. Parker. I'll advise you to be careful, especially with your money."

"Yes, sir."

After glancing at Tara again, the officer headed back to where his patrol car waited. Tara looked up and let out a long, slow breath of relief. "Whew. That was close."

"I know you're not the one he's looking for, Tara." I said.

"What if I am?"

"You mean–"

"Yeah, I'm guilty. I spent the money you gave me at a campground getting a hot shower. After that I got hungry."

I had no idea how to answer that. "Have you been waiting here long?" I asked instead of commenting on her admission.

She stood and picked up a bedraggled backpack. "Since about sunrise. I don't have an alarm clock and didn't want to miss a chance to get outside the city." She pointed toward the retreating Officer Vance. "He seemed to know you."

"I had a run-in with him once before." Tara stared at me with raised eyebrows in an unverbalized question. "Driving after too many beers," I explained. "He helped me get home without reporting me."

Tara shrugged in surprise. "Some cops in the rural area of Wisconsin where I grew up made hassling our commune part of their routine. The adults in the commune calling them 'pigs' probably didn't help any. The cops raided us a few times looking for drugs, usually in the middle of the night. It was scary."

"Did they find any drugs?"

"Only some weed. But since the adults kept their common stash in an outside shed, the cops could never pin possession on any individual. They just confiscated the weed and any money within shouting distance by the principle of civil forfeiture. But I grew up mistrusting the police. Some of the people in our commune had bad experiences with the cops during the 1968 Vietnam war protests in Chicago. Then, once the cops put them in jail, other prisoners abused them. I still get pretty nervous around any law enforcement."

Again, I had no answer but fell back on, "The car is this way." I led her to the decrepit Corolla that had been my transportation for nearly two years. "I'm taking you to the delta of the rivers flowing into Mobile Bay."

Tara got into the car and immediately rolled down the passenger side window despite the hot, humid air surrounding us even early in the morning. "Anywhere outside the city will be fine," she returned.

I drove us down Government Street, through the Bankhead Tunnel, onto the Highway 90 causeway, and past the Battleship Alabama. I attempted to impress her. "My great-grandfather Ezekiel fought for the South in the battle of Mobile Bay." When she didn't show any interest in the war, I didn't add any details I had learned from Dad.

Tara didn't put her head out the window like Ruthie would have done, but I could see her deeply inhaling the non-city air. First, I stopped at Five Rivers Delta Center on an island in the delta and expected to start with Apalachee Exhibit Hall. But nothing could restrain Tara when she saw a sign for a nature trail. "Please stop here," she demanded.

From her backpack, Tara took socks and a pair of worn high-top hiking boots to replace her customary flip-flops. After she changed footwear, I could hardy keep up as she plunged into the bush on her strong legs. Fortunately for me, she stopped frequently to examine nature: lichens on a rock, palmetto leaves with serrated stems, a lizard basking in the morning sun. Alongside the riverbank, Tara pulled a small set of old binoculars out to stare at the v-shaped wake of a brown animal swimming in the water. "Probably a beaver," I suggested.

She corrected me. "Looks like a nutria."

"That's a type of big rat, right?"

"Well it *is* a big rodent," Tara conceded. "Fur farmers introduced the South American coypu to North America. It can be a threat to the environment by burrowing into riverbanks and feeding on native plants. People call them nutrias here, and they're considered an invasive species."

Her comment sounded like one my mother might have made. "How do you know that?"

"I read a lot about nature."

"My ancestors lived close to nature in this area."

"Where was that?"

"The Parkers who pioneered here worked as inland fishermen in the rivers north of the bay. That's still pretty wild country."

"Can we go there?" The higher-pitched voice Tara used to make that appeal sounded like a kid asking to go to a candy store.

* * *

"Most people visit here because of the battlefield," I explained at Blakeley State Park.

"Who had a battle in this remote spot?"

"The Union and Confederacy fought their last major battle here after the Civil War had ended at Appomattox. This is a national historic site. The fight didn't last long. Only about thirty minutes."

"I thought you said your ancestors lived nearby."

"They did live somewhere not far north of here. But we don't know exactly where. Pioneers at that time just built cabins anywhere. Nobody cared. The Parkers camped and fished upriver then brought their catch into the town of Blakeley to sell. As many people lived here as in Mobile at that time. Most people deserted Blakeley in the 1840s because of yellow fever epidemics. Only the ruins are left now."

I looked with trepidation at a brochure that offered sixteen miles of nature trails in Blakeley State Park. I wanted to avoid following Tara over all sixteen miles. "The park map shows some nice boardwalks near the river," I suggested.

"Lead the way, cutie."

Chapter Seventeen

* * *

"This *is* pretty wild and untamed," said Tara looking over the Tensaw River and seemingly endless miles of marshes. Unbroken forests lined the riverbank in both directions. "And dangerous." She pointed to a dark brown snake nearly as thick as my upper arm resting in the sun on a semi-submerged log. "There's a cottonmouth. He and others like him are the reason I wear high-topped boots."

"I'm glad the park provides these boardwalks."

"Me too. But American vipers–cottonmouths, copperheads, and rattlesnakes–aren't aggressive. Studies show that 80% of them can be gently picked up by hand without biting if the snake isn't threatened beforehand. Nearly all bites are the result of people fooling with the snake. Frequently alcohol is involved."

I shuddered. "Remind me not to drink and snake."

Tara laughed. "No kidding." Then she got more serious. "On the Appalachian trail, Bennie and I found a solitary hiker wearing tennis shoes who had been bitten by a copperhead. He'd stepped over a fallen tree trunk and got fanged from behind on the ankle. The copperhead hid underneath the trunk and had been disturbed by the footsteps of previous hikers. Our hiker's foot and leg had swollen up like a beach ball. Bennie stayed with him while I hurried eight miles to where I could call help. That's why you should always step on top of a log. Then the next step will take you out of strike range. Even venomous snakes have enemies, though." She pointed to where an eight-foot gator floated motionless, nearly hidden by some water plants.

Tara continued to stare at the cottonmouth and the alligator. I saw no fear or revulsion, only caution and regard for wild creatures. "And your forefathers lived in this wilderness?" She gestured to the delta and then looked at me with respect for my heritage.

By way of answer, I repeated some of the fishing tales I had heard Dad tell about Daniel Parker and his descendants and the wonders of Mobile Bay. I also described the periodic "jubilee" when crabs, shrimp, eels, and flounders leave deeper waters and swarm into the beach.

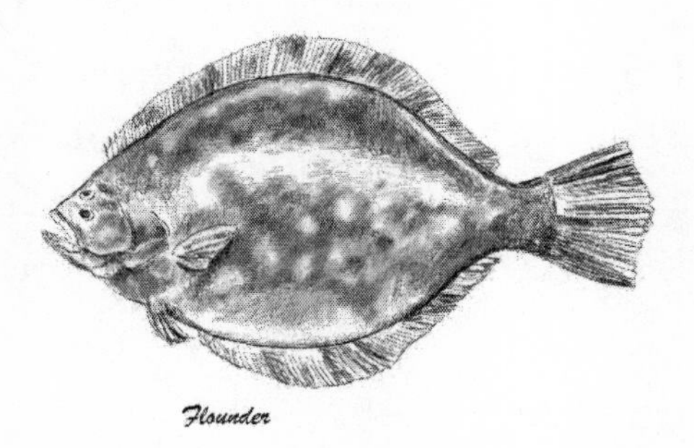

Flounder

"That happens after a cloudy day, right?" asked Tara. "Usually in August about three a.m."

I looked at her with wonder and respect. "How did you know that?"

"I read. Lack of sunlight on the algae in the water causes an oxygen depletion. Have you seen one?"

I shook my head. "No, I've never seen one. The jubilee only happens on the eastern shore and lasts just a few hours. We live on the western shore." I went on to tell Tara about hundred-pound alligator gars and bluefish chasing mullet into the waves breaking onto the beach. "Sometimes, people catch bluefish by kicking them out of the surf onto the sand." Every story about nature and the outdoors interested Tara.

I saw her slap at some gnats that had emerged from the salt grass. "Had enough nature for today?"

"Yes, I have. Thanks for bringing me outside the city, Jeremy."

"How about a late seafood lunch, then?"

"I'd love that."

I could not get over the feeling, *She really likes you,* as I drove us out of the park. Tara was a woman in union with God's creation. A person to be trusted.

Thirty minutes later I pulled into the crushed-oyster-shell parking lot of a ramshackle seafood establishment on the causeway east of Mobile. A few gulls sat on posts of abandoned piers protruding from the water. Pelicans wheeled in the air and periodically dived for mullet. Sailboats plied the tranquil waters. The restaurant had been built on telephone-pole-sized posts.

"Why is the place raised from the ground?" asked Tara.

I parked and turned off the car's engine. "To lift it above possible flood tides. Hurricane winds can push a flood into the bay and onto shore. The pounding waves can destroy nearly anything in their way."

Stepping into the restaurant, we smelled the distinct odor of frying fish and hush puppies. Even to Tara, the air conditioning felt good after the hot humidity outside. Despite its humble exterior, the restaurant's interior predicted a high-class meal. The waiter gave us a table overlooking the bay and handed us plastic laminated menus. "What would you like?" I asked Tara.

"Something Gulf coast. What would you recommend?"

"You could have fried shrimp. Or you could go radical and get something Cajun."

"Cajuns are French-speaking peoples forcibly imported from Acadia by the British, I think. Are the Parkers Cajuns?"

"My great-grandmother was a full-blooded Cajun. That makes me one-eighth Cajun—a Creole. If you want something Cajun with a lot of seafood, you could try the étouffée—a seafood stew served over rice."

Tara, accepting the étouffée, nodded to the listening waiter and handed him the menu. I ordered the shrimp and an appetizer of grilled oysters served with butter and garlic for us to share. "I'll let you try my shrimp," I told her.

Tara acted a bit overwhelmed by the surroundings and my generosity. Dad's unknowing generosity, that is, since I planned on using his credit card. I hardly knew how to begin a dinner conversation with such a beautiful, mature woman. I remembered Tara's knowledge of the origins of Cajuns and tried a compliment while we waited for our dinners. "You know a lot about stuff, like nature and history."

"Hello, I went to college. Three years, anyway. I also like to read and have a lot of time to do so. Long winters in Wisconsin—now days and nights on the road."

Her comment about college reminded me about Mom and Dad's desire for me to attend. "Why did you go to college?"

"You already know that I grew up in a hippie commune. Everybody there wanted to experience Walden Pond."

I only vaguely remembered the book *Walden* from my junior year lit class. "What was that about?"

"A minimalist life, unlimited freedom, no responsibilities. A hippie manifesto. On the commune, everybody, including the kids, did pretty much what they wanted to do. Not many people wanted to work like serfs in the fields or master the technology needed to run a productive farm. They raised hardly enough produce to feed everyone, much less sell to get money and pay for things like electricity. And–as I told you–the cops occasionally took whatever money the group had."

Tara idly chewed on a fingernail as she reminisced. "At age fifteen, what I wanted to do was take a hot shower, get some school clothes that didn't look like Goodwill had rejected them, and eat something better than boiled potatoes and peas."

Our appetizer of grilled oysters arrived. I divided them between us, four and four. "So what did you do about that?"

Tara laughed. "I stenciled a few signs that said 'Visit a Hippie Commune - $20.'" Her hand gestured to each word on an imaginary sign. "Then I nailed them to telephone poles on the highway that passed us. I put up arrows to show the way. Within an hour, tourists on their way to Madison followed the signs up our driveway. I met the cars and collected twenty dollars per carload for a tour. These are wonderful," Tara interrupted herself after trying a grilled oyster.

We savored the oysters silently a few minutes before I prompted Tara again. "What did the others at the commune think about you putting them on display?"

"Some complained at first. Others labeled me a 'bourgeois capitalist.' Then I paid the electric bill to restore our power, bought a chainsaw to cut firewood, got a new distributer for the tractor, and treated everybody to store-bought ice cream. The complaints stopped for a while."

"Wow! That's remarkable," I said as our entrées arrived.

"You haven't heard the best part yet," said Tara as she sampled the étouffée. "I love this! Just enough spice to magnify the tastes of the seafood."

"After being dumped in the low country of what's now Louisiana, the Cajun people had to learn how to live on the food they could catch—even things like crayfish and alligators. They developed a unique and spicy cuisine." I forked over a batter-fried shrimp. "Try this non-Cajun southern food."

Tara's eyes widened as she tried the shrimp. "I love this, too."

"Just eat all you want of everything."

"That might not leave anything for you."

I repeated my juvenile prayer as a joke. "We thank you Father, Son, and Holy Ghost. Whoever eats the fastest gets the most."

Tara laughed. "That was reality, not a joke, at the commune."

"You were about to tell me the best part," I reminded her. "And how did you get from the commune to college?"

"Oh, yeah. The best part is still coming." Tara continued her tale while eating. I let her have most of my shrimp and the étouffée while I filled up on hush puppies, French fries, and bread. She talked between bites. "More and more cars with tourists kept coming. A few of my fellow commune family members tried to horn in on my success. So I started to embellish my tour stories. Hearing about easy sex and drugs fascinated the tourists. The commune was, in fact, mostly drudgery and deprivation. But I made up outrageous stories to give the customers what they wanted. I threw in some communist jargon and told the tourists the hippies called each other 'comrade' when no outsiders could hear.

"Many started leaving me tips, sometimes a hundred dollars, in addition to the twenty. Then I added a twist by saying that any tips beyond the twenty dollars would go to my college fund. I told the tourists that going to college would be my escape from the sex- and drug-infested commune. With an education I could make something of my life. I even cut my hair short and dressed like a preppie trapped among the hippies. The tourists believed my stories because they made them feel morally superior. A few even offered to rescue me by taking me with them.

"A news station in Madison picked up the story of a teenaged girl trapped at a commune but trying to make good. Then a station in Chicago sent a reporter. Stations in other cities followed. Following the publicity, tourists and money rolled in. Eventually my scheme exceeded the hippies' limits of do-anything-you-want freedom. My fanciful stories brought another drug raid. Child welfare workers showed up asking questions. And the steaks I had bought didn't please the vegetarians. The other commune members banished me at age seventeen. My own mother voted to oust me. But I had collected enough cash for college. *Why not suck it up and go?* I asked myself. So I did escape, in that sense, just didn't make something of my life the way the tourists expected. Most of the other commune residents also bailed out as they got older and missed some of the luxuries I had provided.

"I liked learning at college and taking hot showers in the dorm. Plus I had a natural talent for theatrics. But I never quite fit in with the undergraduate party culture. A lot of the men thought coming from a commune would make me an easy mark. Then a tenured teacher started trying to hit on me. Although I complained to the campus police, they claimed to believe the teacher's denial. I dropped out a semester before graduation in protest."

We had finished dinner. I paid the bill and led the way back to the car. Tara continued talking as we drove back to the park where I had met her. Not wishing the day to be over, I parked on the far side, requiring us to walk together back to her bench. As Tara rambled on about the disillusionment of college, her dropping out, adventures on the road, and the places she'd been, I took another long look at her. Never had I seen a more beautiful, wild, and carefree creature. A holder of the secrets of life.

I heard myself ask, "Tara, would you go to my prom with me?"

Chapter Eighteen

* * *

Tara stopped talking and turned toward me. "You're still in high school?" A look of bemusement covered her face. "You're asking me to your high school prom?"

My spirit wilted. How could I have invited such a sophisticated, mature woman to a teenage dance, even if it *was* a prom? "Never mind," I tried to recover. "That was just an impulse. You're way too good for that."

Tara paused for a long minute, considering my proposal. "Why not go with you? A high school prom could be a hoot. Nobody asked me, the hippie girl, to my own prom."

My heart soared at the same time my tongue froze. Having spoken on an impulse, I had no follow-up words prepared. I didn't need any. Tara continued, "I don't have anything to wear, though. This is the best I have." She opened her arms to emphasize her shorts and athletic top.

My tongue regained some mobility. "What would a dress cost?"

"Maybe a hundred dollars."

I didn't have a hundred dollars. But I did have Dad's credit card and the pin number.

"This way," I pointed to where I knew we'd find an ATM. Standing in front, I inserted the card and entered the pin.

"I'll need shoes, too," Tara added. "And some makeup." Overcome with joy, I added another fifty dollars to the hundred.

* * *

"Who are you taking to the prom?" Mom asked when I asked for money to rent a tuxedo. Dad listened nearby with interest.

I didn't look at my parents. "A girl I met."

"I thought maybe you'd ask Giselle from church."

"No, not Giselle."

"That's too bad."

You don't know Giselle, Mom, I thought.

"Do we know the girl's parents?"

"I doubt it."

* * *

I had told Mom and Dad that my prom date would meet me at our house that Saturday night. They hovered anxiously as I waited for Tara to arrive. Our front doorbell rang. Opening the door, I stood stunned. Tara waited on the doorstep, wearing her smile. And that's not all she wore. She had on a red nightclub dress with thin shoulder straps. The dress ended about mid-thigh, showing her long legs. The neckline plunged toward her navel. The dress appeared to have been shrink-fitted onto her. Either that or not finding her size, she had been forced into a dress too small. With shiny black heels, she looked back at me almost eye level. And I had grown to six feet. Tara's soft reddish-brown curls, released from the braid, tumbled down her bare back. Dark red lipstick and dangling gold-colored earrings highlighted her striking features.

"Nice tux," she said.

"Uh, you look amazing. Beautiful dress."

"Surprising what you can get at Goodwill, huh?"

At my gesture, Tara stepped over the threshold. Ruthie ran up wagging her entire body. Tara leaned over to take the dog's muzzle in her hands and stroke Ruthie's head. "I love dogs."

"These are my parents, Dave and Katie Parker," I managed to gasp. "Mom and Dad, this is Tara."

Dad offered his hand and spoke first. "Glad to meet you. What's your last name, Tara?"

Tara firmly shook the extended hand. "Grabowski, Dave. I use my mother's surname. My father is a Kennedy." At my parents' stunned expression, she amended, "Just kidding. The man my mother thinks is my father is named Gnarly Harkness."

I could see my mother clenching her teeth over my date's appearance and demeanor. Tara likely noticed but proceeded. "You have a lovely home, Katie. I'd like to have a house someday. Right now, I'm living in a van. Easy to move around that way. I parked it in your driveway. I hope that's okay."

Tara's use of my parents' first names unnerved me a little. But not as much as Tara's reference to the van.

Mom made her jaws move. "Thank you, Tara. Welcome to our home. Jeremy has lived all of his life here."

Tara abandoned her smile in favor of a broad grin. "He's fortunate to have had such a nice place to grow up."

I had a corsage ready. But Tara's tiny dress straps didn't look adequate to hold it. Mom produced a red ribbon for Tara's wrist. She then took the corsage and pinned it to the ribbon.

Dad also rose to the occasion. "Sweetheart, we should let these kids go." He picked up the waiting camera. "You two stand together by the stairs. Okay. One, two, three." He snapped the photo and looked at it on the screen. "Now another one of you two by the door."

The pictures made, Dad handed me the keys to Mom's car. "Why don't you take our car, Son. Tara's van will be fine in the driveway. You kids have a good time. Try to not stay out all night, Jeremy."

Once in the car, Tara laughed. "Wow! You were right about your parents being old-fashioned. That was like stepping into a 1950s TV show."

Every eye turned to look when I brought Tara into the prom. She made my female classmates look like girls pretending to be women. Most of them had loosely fitting floor-length evening dresses compared to Tara's tight and short nightclub dress.

The guys and girls tended to clump into separate groups at all school functions, even prom. In this case, the tux-wearing guys all clumped around me. That is, around my date. Even Mr. Pritchard, our economics and government teacher who had suspended me, sidled over for a closer look.

I left Tara surrounded by male admirers and hurried to get her some punch. The punch bowl reeked of alcohol. Guys had spiked it hoping to get their dates drunk. Most of the girls played along, pretending not to notice. I returned to the throng admiring my date in time to notice someone showing her a pack of cigarettes and asking, "Would you like to go outside for a smoke?"

Tara grimaced, "Ugh! No thanks. I want only fresh air in my lungs." She tasted the spiked punch and set it aside. "Do they have a soft drink table here? I'd like a coke." I hurried to meet that need.

The hired DJ called everyone to the dance floor as I handed Tara her coke. She gulped it in several swallows. In a brazen move, Brody the football star asked my date to dance. Mr. Pritchard looked like he'd like the second dance.

"Sorry, fella. Every dance is promised to my boyfriend." She put her hand on my arm and pulled me toward the dance floor. "When you've got a horse, you ride it," Tara said over her shoulder to her admirers. The guys dispersed to find their dates. Mr. Pritchard returned to his observation perch.

"Let's start with a slow dance," shouted the DJ.

Slow dance? My heart sank. I clasped Tara's right hand with my left. I put my right hand lightly on her hip. She responded by reaching around my waist and pulling me close. Tara crushed our bodies together from our hips to our collar bones. She put her head under my chin as we took tiny steps and swayed gently to the music. I looked over her head to see Giselle staring at me. She was in the arms of Brody, who for the time being had given up trying to steal my date.

The following dances sped up in tempo. Tara stole the show, writhing in time with the music, dancing around me, and making me look good.

After an hour or so of dancing, Tara leaned close to me. "Have you had enough prom, Jeremy Parker? Ready to leave?"

If nothing else, living with Mom and Dad had taught me one thing: "Quit while you're ahead." I thought, *Nothing could possibly make this prom any better.*

"I'm ready," I whispered back.

"Don't go," a male voice beseeched us as we headed toward the exit.

"Sorry," Tara answered with a voice that nearly all could hear. "I want Jeremy all to myself for a while."

Chapter Nineteen

* * *

In the car I asked, "Where did you learn to dance like that?"

Tara gave the wry smile that made her so irresistible. "At college. All theater majors are taught to dance." Then she started laughing. "I was right. Your prom *was* a hoot." Turning to me and smiling she asked, "Isn't that the type of prom date you wanted?"

Then I realized what she had done. "You were acting, right? Playing a role for me?"

"Remember I studied theater before chucking the whole scene. Thank you for taking me to your prom, Jeremy. That was sweet."

I truly loved her then for the first time.

* * *

As we drove away, Tara scoffed at my classmates. "Those boys back at your prom are just like the ones at my college. They think drinking and smoking makes them mature. They only reveal their immaturity. They're just crowd-followers. It's so pathetic."

I nodded. "I agree with you."

Tara scooted over on the car seat to sit close to me. "I'm glad you're not like them, Jeremy."

"You're not like anybody I've ever met."

"Thank you. But I've got a confession to make. I only paid forty dollars for this dress and ten dollars for the shoes. With some of the money you gave me, I bought us some herbal tea."

"Tea?"

"It'll relax us after the prom. Would you like some?"

"Sure."

"Okay, then. We'll need some hot water. Find a truck stop."

Interstate 65 passing through Mobile had several truck stops. Within a few minutes, I pulled into one of the parking lots. "Go inside and get us each a big cup of hot water," Tara instructed.

When I returned with scalding water, Tara dropped a hefty pinch of dry leaves and a glob of coconut oil into each cup. "This will take a couple of minutes to brew. Drive us to someplace where we'll have a view over the bay."

I took us to a turnoff on the causeway overlooking the lighted battleship *Alabama*. The lights of Mobile formed a background. A nearly full moon hung in the sky. The moon shined through fluffy cumulous clouds, making them appear luminescent against the starry sky. There we sat sipping the tea. Tara talked about all the places she would like to go and adventures to pursue. I started to feel more relaxed. Apparently she had relaxed too, because her words slowed. "Tell me more about your life and family," she prompted.

I found myself repeating Dad's stories about pioneers, soldiers, and fishermen. I told about the regional trips I had taken with Mom and Dad the previous summer. She laughed and enjoyed all my stories. I experienced a pleasant euphoria in her presence unlike any feeling before. *This is what it's like to be in love,* I told myself. Soon we were laughing giddily at the silliest things. I then noticed how bright the stars sparkled and how Tara radiated indescribable beauty.

I leaned over to kiss her, which she returned with passion—kisses unlike the tender kisses I had shared with Giselle.

After a few minutes of intense kissing, Tara asked, "Are you hungry?"

I discovered that I felt starved. "Let's find someplace to eat," I suggested.

An all-night restaurant seemed a good place to both of us. I ordered large steaks and lobster for each of us. Except they didn't have lobster. Somehow that seemed funny and we giggled until the harried waitress brought our steaks, huge baked potatoes, and fresh hot bread. As we devoured the steaks, I told Tara the story about feeding Zeek my tennis shoe. Heads in the restaurant turned to watch Tara laughing uproariously.

Then Tara became a little more serious. "Jeremy, you're a bit young. But you're cute and sweet. We could have a lot of fun together. You'll graduate high school soon. Would you like to go on the road with me?"

"Where would I sleep?"

"In the van, silly." The implication renewed our giggling.

"We're not married," I managed between swallowing and laughing.

"So what? My parents never married. Marriage is just a gimmick to tie people down."

I felt a powerful urge. Like none ever before. Tara would be worth any sacrifice. I could imagine myself traveling with her. Being with her in every way.

After eating, we began to unwind a little. By now the time had passed 3:00 a.m. and I felt sleepy. After leaving the restaurant, I turned the car toward home. In Mom and Dad's driveway, Tara spoke more seriously. "Can you get any money?"

"I have more than $30,000 in my college fund."

My comment animated Tara. "Wow! We could get a long way on that. We'd have a world of fun. We could go to California and stop at the Grand Canyon. I read that you can hike to the bottom and back in a day. We could take old Route 66 and visit Roswell where people say aliens landed. Then we'd explore Canada and Alaska. We might even take a cruise someplace."

Everything she said sounded wonderful. Having obeyed Mom for all my life, Tara taking charge of our future seemed quite natural. But unlike Mom, Tara needed me. And I needed her. We would help each other.

Outside the car, Tara gave me the most passionate kiss of all. I was ready for the van right then and started to get in. Tara held my arm and pulled me back. "Hold on, fella. You get the money. Then we'll hit the road together." She left in her van while I watched.

* * *

Inside the house I found Mom and Dad waiting up for me even though the clock showed 4:00 a.m.

Mom started right in. "Jeremy, that girl isn't good for you."

"Who are you to say who's good for me? And Tara needs me. The Bible says we're supposed to help people, doesn't it?"

"That girl cares for nobody but herself."

"That isn't true. She cares about the environment."

Mom responded, "No, your father is an environmentalist. He gets involved. That girl probably just talks about it."

I hadn't heard Tara mention any actual activism, so tried a different argument. "Ruthie liked Tara."

"Ruthie likes everybody."

Dad spoke for the first time. "I liked Tara too, Son. But that doesn't mean she's right for you."

"Who is right for me?"

"How about Giselle?" Mom suggested.

"Tara doesn't smoke and drink, unlike the girls from our church. Like Giselle. And Giselle's not exactly moral either."

This accusation set Mom back. She spoke more cautiously, "There are some nice girls out there."

"I don't know any nicer than Tara. She appreciates me. Unlike everybody else. Unlike you."

At this point Dad stepped closer to me. He looked carefully into my eyes before speaking more calmly. "What about you, Son? Did you smoke or drink anything tonight?"

"Nothing bad. All we had was a little hot tea."

"Did you use tea bags?"

"No, Tara had some special herbal tea leaves."

"Uh-huh. You better go to bed and get some sleep."

* * *

I woke gradually late Sunday afternoon with the most wonderful feeling. I thought about Tara and her offer all day. *Did I dream about the new and exciting life I could have with Tara?* Remembering the argument with my parents convinced me I wasn't dreaming. All I would need to do is finish the last days of high school without doing anything stupid. But who intends to learn anything two days from high school graduation? Certainly, I didn't—not when the most beautiful and vivacious woman in the world was waiting for me.

Dad kept a box of spare keys inside Mom's grandfather clock. After breakfast on Monday morning, while Mom fed Ruthie, I groped in the dark until my fingers touched the box. Quicker than I had imagined, the keys to the cabin cruiser, Audit, were in my hand.

"I'm off to school, Mom," I shouted.

"Okay, honey. I'm sorry again about the argument we had after your prom. Your father and I were just surprised."

"Forget it."

"Have a nice day, Jeremy."

But West Side High would not be the school I attended that day.

*   *   *

I found Tara's van parked unobtrusively in the same parking lot where I'd seen it before. Her bleary face appeared at the driver's side window in response to my tapping on the door.

Tara rolled down the window. "Hi, fella. To what do I owe this very early morning surprise?"

"How about an adventure today?" I jangled Audit's keys in front of her. "Would you like a boat ride?"

Tara wiped sleep from her eyes, opened the van door, and stepped onto the pavement. Apparently, she slept in the same shorts and athletic top she'd worn at the park. "Don't you have two more days of school?"

"What are they going to do? Expel me?"

She gave me the wry smile I adored. "I guess not," she said. "I'll need a couple of minutes."

I tried to project calm confidence and a flirtations touch. "We've got all day, beautiful."

I hadn't pictured Tara as a morning sleepyhead. Somehow that endeared her more to me. I had learned something about her private life, something intimate. She turned back to the van and selected several items to stuff into her backpack. "I'll need some coffee," she said. "How about a McDonald's or someplace?" She collected her loose hair into a bushy ponytail.

After refreshing herself in a McDonald's restroom then downing two cups of hot coffee and an Egg McMuffin, the Tara I knew reemerged. "So, Jeremy Parker, what sort of boat ride are we going on?"

"Let's stop by a grocery store to get some food for the day. Then we'll see where the boat takes us."

"Lead the way, cutie."

Chapter Twenty

* * *

At the marina, I led Tara to Audit's berth. Between us we carried the food, ice, and sodas we had purchased at the grocery store. I went into the bait and tackle shop to purchase some frozen herring to use for bait. Returning to the berth, I found Tara surrounded by a web-footed audience. The birds reminded me of the boys around her at prom. Except in this case, the birds appreciated the bread Tara freely distributed rather than her appearance.

"That's our lunch," I protested.

Tara threw out the last handful of crumbs from a loaf of bread. Sea gulls struggled to grab every piece. "It's their lunch now. We still have the crackers."

I saw Tara look at the brown pelicans waiting beyond the squawking gulls. Then she glanced at the paper bag that held the lunch meat we had bought for our sandwiches.

"Pelicans want fish, not ham," I told her while keeping the herring hidden.

"They sure are big birds, aren't they? Do they really carry fish in that pouch under their bill?"

"Only if their stomachs are full and they can't swallow anymore."

Using a key taken from the grandfather clock, I unlocked the cable securing Audit to the dock. Tara effortlessly stepped on board the bobbing boat. To my slight disappointment, no "Hold my hand" from this woman.

"Shouldn't we check out with the marina, or something?" she asked.

"No. They don't care where we go," I lied. In truth, I had misgivings about what Charlie, the manager, might say about my taking out the boat without Dad. *Better that we get away without speaking to anyone,* I convinced myself. Plus, I didn't see Charlie or anyone else for that matter. The marina was quiet for such a beautiful day. I internally rejoiced. *No observers to ask questions I don't want to answer.*

The ignition key started the inboard motor. The odor of diesel fuel came from the exhaust. Without asking, Tara took the initiative to throw off the ropes holding Audit to the dock. I pushed the throttle into reverse and backed out of the berth.

A few minutes of idle speed to exit the marina, then we surged into Mobile Bay. I pushed the throttle forward to propel us across the slightly choppy water. "Where do you want to go?" I shouted above the motor noise.

Tara stood on the back deck from where we normally fished reveling in the wide sky and outdoor experience. With her feet spread for balance, Tara closed her eyes, and lifted her arms above her in a V. I imagined her as a Greek goddess in command of her destiny and the fates of ordinary men.

After standing with uplifted arms for a minute, Tara took her backpack into the tiny cabin. Then she came back wearing a pink bikini. Forget about voluptuous women or skinny delicate women in a bathing suit. What's hot is a woman with strong arms and legs and a taut body. I remembered girlish Giselle in the two-piece swimsuit at the lake. *We were just kids then,* I thought.

Tara reached into her backpack and pulled out some sunscreen. I watched as she applied the lotion on her arms and legs.

"Here, put some on my back," she said.

"I'd have done your arms and legs, too," I said.

"Settle down there, fella." Tara stood still as I used my right hand to rub her back while my left steered the boat. Her skin felt warm and firm. The sweet odor of the lotion filled the air.

Once lotioned up, Tara started exploring the boat, even edging along the side to the front. She dangled her bare legs on either side of the bow. "Why is the water brown?" she shouted.

"It's tannin and soil from the rivers flowing into Mobile Bay. I'll take us to clearer water." I steered toward some of the sandbars along the coast. I pointed toward the east shore. "Over there, my grandfather Parker started an oyster bed on a shallow mud flat in the early 1950s. He sank some old junk and threw in shells he had collected behind a restaurant. The oysters just came to where they could attach to something solid. We don't legally own the bed. But we don't tell anyone where it is, either."

"I liked the oysters we had in the restaurant. Can we catch some of those?" Tara asked.

"I've got an idea you'll like better." Dark gray backs breaking the water's surface caught my attention. I turned Audit slightly to intercept a pod of dolphins. They swam alongside and ahead of us, seeming to enjoy our company.

"Dolphins are my favorite animal," Tara shouted. She hung over the side trying to touch one. "Can I swim with them?"

"You can try." With that encouragement, Tara threw herself into the water from the moving boat. I turned Audit around to find her treading water and looking around. But the dolphins, unused to direct human contact, continued in the direction we had been traveling.

I imagined Tara as a dolphin. A strong young animal. Perfectly at ease in her environment.

"One brushed my leg," Tara said as she climbed up the boat's ladder. I noticed the dolphin earrings she was wearing. "That was totally awesome," she said as she released her wet hair from her ponytail to dry. "What next?" she asked.

* * *

Forty-five minutes later I beached Audit on a sandbar. "Have you ever been crabbing?" I asked.

"No. And I haven't eaten crab, either."

"It's like lobster, only sweeter."

"How will we catch them?"

"With a net." I went into the cabin and pulled a long-handled net from its storage spot. Returning to the deck, I found Tara already standing on the sandy beach.

"Look, I see one!" She pointed into the water and turned her head to see if I saw it, too. Her eyes returned to where the crab had been. "It's gone. Where did the crab go?"

I jumped down from the boat with the net and a plastic bucket. "It's hiding in the sand. Look for another one and keep your eye on it."

Together we walked barefoot in the clear shallow water surrounding the sandbar. Tara pointed. "There's another one."

A blue crab sidled away from us in foot-deep water. "Watch it," I told her as we approached.

Tara gasped to see the crab burrow under a layer of sand in an instant.

I handed her the net. "Now scoop up the sand where you saw the crab disappear."

Tara leaned into the handle and with her strong arms pushed the net into the sand where she last saw the crab. She lifted. The sand drained away, leaving the crab struggling in the net. "I got him. I got him."

I held out the bucket. "Dump him in here. But watch your fingers."

Tara looked at the crab in the bucket. "Looks like a big insect."

"They taste great, though."

"How will we cook them?"

"We can boil them. There's a propane stove in the cabin. Let's see if we can get a few more."

* * *

Two hours later, Tara sucked the meat from a leg of the last of seven crabs. "That's better than lobster. I'd do this every day if I lived here and owned a boat."

I imagined Tara as a carefree Tahitian woman on a tropical island. The more time I spent with Tara, the more I realized this was the kind of life I wanted to live, too—no worries or responsibilities, full of fun and adventure. Maybe this version of me—the person I was when I was with Tara—was my true self, the one I had been trying to find.

"Actually, crabs are out of season right now. But nobody will miss these few." Privately I exalted in being a rule-breaker in front of Tara.

She nodded appreciatively and threw the shells to a nearby flock of seagulls that had discovered us. The birds somehow consumed the remains, shell and all.

"Would you like to catch some fish?"

"I'd love to."

As we motored toward the offshore reefs, I pointed to the side of the inlet by Fort Morgan. "That's where the Union and Confederacy fought the Battle of Mobile Bay." I waved toward the open ocean. "Out there, Dad and I caught a sailfish."

"This place is really a part of you, isn't it, Jeremy? I'll bet that if cut, you'd bleed brown bay water."

"My family has been living here for 200 years. But I want to get away. To see the world."

"Have you thought more about going on the road with me after you graduate?"

"Hardly about anything else. And I'm ready. If you'll come to the auditorium, tomorrow night, we can leave straight from my graduation."

"All right, I'll have the van running." Tara paused before speaking. "You said something about some money. Maybe $30,000?"

"Yeah. My college funds. I'll bring the money."

"In cash?"

"Okay, in cash."

"Good. We can have a lot of fun with that. Let me brew us some more herbal tea to celebrate."

* * *

"Usually we get a few bites by now." I stared into the water as Audit drifted over one of the offshore artificial reefs. "Below us fish congregate around junk cars, old oil rigs, useless farm equipment, and even obsolete army tanks the state sank to make an artificial reef. Sometimes fish sense weather changes, barometric pressure or something, and won't take any bait." Two empty cups remained where we had enjoyed some of Tara's tea.

"That's okay. I'm just enjoying being outdoors. And with you, Jeremy."

Tara reached out to caress my arm. In response, I rubbed her knee. She leaned over to take my earlobe in her teeth. I turned my head to receive a kiss–a kiss that started affectionately and developed into passion. After a few minutes of making out, Tara whispered in my ear, "Maybe we should go into the cabin."

In the cabin we struggled to lie down together on one of the narrow bunks. In an awkward position, we resumed kissing. Tara shifted herself to lie on top of me. A tilt of the boat threw her off me and onto the floor. Both of us laughed. I heard wind whipping the canopy over the bridge. I attempted to get off the bunk to help Tara off the floor, but the increased pitching of the boat made standing difficult. Sunshine no longer came in through the tiny view ports. As the sky darkened and the wind started to rise, the first splatters of rain smashed onto the windows.

"Let me check something," I told Tara once she had crawled back onto the bunk. I returned to the deck and my eyes widened at the sight of a towering black wall of clouds blocking the horizon in the west. A few flashes of lighting arced down from the upper layers of the clouds.

Chapter Twenty-One

* * *

"Are we going to have rain?" asked Tara.

I turned to see her standing beside me, looking at the approaching front. "Maybe more than rain."

I switched on the boat's radio and dialed to the marine weather channel to hear, "The small craft advisory issued this morning has been upgraded to a small craft alert. All boats should remain off the bay. Severe weather is approaching with strong winds, hail, and possible embedded tornadoes. This is the same front that spawned several funnel clouds in Biloxi earlier this morning. All craft should be advised."

"That doesn't sound good," said Tara. She pointed at the black wall of clouds. "Is that what they're talking about?"

"I think so. We need to go back now and fast," I answered.

"Okay."

But going back wasn't so easy. We had to get back into the bay before we could get off the bay. At full throttle Audit labored against the wind and six-foot waves. The tide going out didn't help either. Wind rushing from under the black wall of clouds made me shiver. Tara went into the cabin to change out of her bikini.

Back on the deck she pointed in the direction we were heading. "What's that?"

A thin waterspout danced across the bay in front of us. I grabbed the microphone on the boat's radio. Not knowing what to say, I mimicked what I'd seen on TV. "Mayday. Mayday. Can anyone hear us?"

A dispassionate voice came back. "Identify yourself. Are you on the open water?"

"This is the Audit from Mobile. We're east of Dauphin Island. We can see a tornado."

The wall of black clouds swept over us. Lighting flashed continuously. Furious rain made the entire world gray. Nickle-sized hail stung our skin and collected on the deck. Waves pitched the Audit wildly.

We could capsize, I realized.

"Tara, Dad keeps life preservers under the bunks in the cabin. Get them," I yelled over the tumult. Alarm showed on her face.

I shouted into the mic. "We're in the middle of the storm. I can't see anything. We might capsize."

"This is the United States Coast Guard. We have your signal triangulated. A rescue ship is being dispatched from the Dauphin

Island station to your location. Put on your life preservers. If your craft capsizes, jump clear so that you're not entangled in anything. Then try to remain at that location by swimming to the boat and clinging to the hull."

I felt somebody pulling on my arms. Tara had put on a life preserver and was trying to put one on me. "Hold still," she ordered.

"Stay on the deck!" I told her. "That way if the boat flips you won't be trapped in the cabin." I could tell by Tara's expression that she was afraid. I didn't try to visualize how my face looked.

Twenty eternally long minutes later, we heard a siren and then saw a flashing light through the pouring rain and wind. A thunderous speaker stated, "This is the Coast Guard. Prepare for a tow."

Despite our instructions to remain topside, Tara darted into the cabin. She emerged with her backpack and a couple of one-pound lead fishing sinkers. She put the sinkers into the backpack and threw it all overboard. She saw me looking at her in surprise. "Coast Guard is part of law enforcement, right? We wouldn't want them to catch us with marijuana, would we?"

In response to my puzzled stare, she added, "What did you think that herbal tea was?"

I didn't answer, but caught a line thrown from the Coast Guard ship. I secured the line to Audit's bow.

The waves seemed less intense in the wake made by the powerful engines of the fifty-four-foot ship. For a minute, I considered that maybe we could have made it on our own. But not having made it would have meant a catastrophe, maybe our deaths. Forty minutes later the Coast Guard left us at the marina. The worst of the storm had abated. A uniformed Coast Guard representative met us on the dock.

"I need your pilot's license, sir," he demanded.

"I don't have one," I admitted.

"Then why did you take a boat out, especially with a small craft advisory in effect? You got caught in a micro-burst. You're lucky that twister didn't get you."

I had no answer but handed over my Alabama driver's license. The Coast Guard officer looked at my license then up at Tara. "Okay, I understand. But that's no excuse. Whose boat is this?"

"My father's. David Parker."

The Coast Guard officer shook his head while writing down Audit's registration number and recording the information from my driver's license. "We're required to report this to the proper authorities of the State of Alabama. They'll deal with your violations of state maritime regulations. I would expect a heavy fine."

Neither threat concerned me. In just one more day, I expected to be away from Mobile and from Alabama.

Leading Tara back to my car in the drizzling rain, I expected her to be upset, perhaps even angry.

"Wow! That was great, Jeremy. What a hoot!"

I looked at her. "Weren't you scared?"

She gave me her wry smile. "Sure, for a while. But I felt alive, too." She summarized, "We didn't die. And we didn't get arrested. What more can you ask for such an adventure in the outdoors? I only wish I'd remembered to take my binoculars out of the backpack."

There it was. Tara's secret to life. Avoid the worst consequences and don't care about the rest!

"See you tomorrow night," she said when I dropped her off at the van.

* * *

Everybody simply goes through the motions the last day before high school graduation. The kids going to college have their acceptances all sewn up. Those planning to start working know where they'll be. The teachers are eager to be rid of another class of dunderheads. Nobody cares anymore. Just finish the year out without doing something stupid, get the graduation over, turn in your gown, and get on with life.

Me? I had nothing planned until the opportunity of a thousand lifetimes fell into my lap. That night I would graduate and be done with West Side High School. The next day I'd be living free on the road with Tara—the most beautiful and fun woman in the entire world. My course had been determined. That's why a summons to the principal's office confounded me.

The office secretary showed me into the principal's office. There I found not Mr. Snyder, but my father. For once in my lifetime his face did not light up when seeing me. He looked like a man facing death.

"Dad? What are you doing—"

Uncharacteristically, he interrupted me. "I needed to talk to you, Jeremy. This is probably the last time we'll talk before you become an adult responsible for your own actions—your own future."

"If this is about Tara—"

Dad interrupted again as if he had no time for baloney. "It's about more than Tara, Son. I want you to think clearly about what you're doing. The bank manager called me. He said that you'd withdrawn your college fund in cash. Because you're eighteen and my son, he assumed the best and gave you the money before checking with me."

I started talking when he took a breath. "I know you and Mom intended that money for college. But I don't have the grades or test scores to get into a good school."

"Trust me, Jeremy. You can go to college, if you want to. But let me remind you that a 529 plan set up for college expenses remains legally my money. I could sue you to regain it."

"Maybe so. But you and Mom always called that my money. You intended it for my education. You didn't specify what kind of education."

"We assumed you knew that the money was for college." Being an accountant, Dad had to add, "If the money is spent on anything but college, the earnings are taxable and there's a ten percent penalty."

I had no answer to that but knew that in a few hours I'd be away with Tara. I couldn't allow anything to interfere with that dream.

Sensing my resolve, Dad sighed deeply. "Son, each moment divides our lives into before and after. Be careful when the moment will divide your life into never before and always after."

That sobered me a bit. "Dad, I want to get away from here. To experience some adventures. I don't want to spend years studying books and then just settle into a boring job here in Mobile."

I could tell that my indictment of Dad's life and rejection of his choices hurt him. "I'm sorry, Dad. I didn't mean . . ."

"That's all right, Son. I just want the best for you for an entire lifetime. Have the courage to do the smart thing rather than what seems immediately exciting. Maximize your life for the long haul, not just a few enjoyable years. Please don't rule college out. You may find that college itself is quite an adventure. An education can open a world of new experiences. And a job can be very satisfying, if you remember what and who you're working for."

We sat in silence for several minutes. I couldn't help but recall the good times we had shared fishing. I thought about when his dull job had saved the Hobbses from financial ruin and given them their dream. I thought about the relationship he and Mom had shared through ups and downs for three decades. Then I remembered Tara in the red dress and how much fun we had kissing and laughing together after the prom and on the boat.

Without looking Dad in the eye, I said, "Well, I need to get back to class. We have a graduation rehearsal starting in a few minutes."

"One last thing," he said. "You'll always be my son. And I'll always love you."

I nodded but didn't speak as I walked out the door.

* * *

"What are you doing, Jeremy?" Mom asked after following me to my bedroom when I went home after the day's last class.

"I'm just packing a few things."

She looked from me to the backpack I had stuffed with outdoor clothes, my toothbrush, other toiletries, and some camping supplies. She saw my sleeping bag rolled up and ready. "Are you going somewhere with that girl? With Tara?"

"She's not just that girl, Mom. I love Tara."

Mom remained silent for a minute. "Maybe you do, after a fashion. But does she love you? Real love involves commitment to a lifetime together."

"You and Dad had to take marriage classes to learn to love each other."

"No. We took the classes because we love each other and because we love you. The classes taught us how to live together. How to have fun as a family."

Privately I had to admit that Mom and Dad had done what they needed to do to keep their relationship strong. In my eyes, theirs had been a boring relationship compared to the fun I could have with Tara. But a lot of my friends' parents' relationships hadn't lasted like Mom and Dad's. Then I thought about all the exciting places Tara said that we'd go together. Places I'd only heard about. I picked up my backpack and sleeping bag to go.

Mom blocked my path out of my bedroom. "Jeremy, I know some of the local girls have disappointed you. Please hold out for a true love that can last a lifetime."

"Tara loves me."

"Are you sure?"

I felt a little anger at Mom's insinuation. She had made a difficult decision even worse. I kissed her on the cheek and stepped around her.

"Your father and I will be at your graduation tonight," she called as I went down the stairs.

Chapter Twenty-Two

* * *

Tara and I had agreed for her to bring the van to graduation. As soon as I got my diploma and they pronounced the benediction, I would meet her outside. She had explained her plan, "I'll fill the radiator to the top with water. Then the van should be able to get us to Biloxi before the engine overheats. We can get another radiator there tomorrow morning. Then we're off to California!"

The graduation dragged on with tedious talks and admonitions about changing the world and fulfilling our individual potentials. All the time I thought about spending that night in the van with Tara and drinking some more herbal tea. Thoughts of Dad's words about the value of education for "the long haul" and Mom's talk of "true love" kept intruding.

The graduates with high alphabet names stood to walk across the stage, shake hands with Principal Snyder, and receive their diplomas. As the graduates paraded, memories of Mom and Dad and thoughts of Tara swirled in my mind. A couple of graduates crossing the stage pulled some high jinx—one gymnast walked off the stage on her hands, a guy put on a red clown nose—once they had the diploma in their hand. I only wanted graduation to be over. Finally, the emcee called the *P*s starting with Parker. I walked straight across the stage, mindful that somewhere in the audience Mom and Dad were watching as Tara waited outside. Finally, the ceremony ended. My classmates cheered, hugged, and gave each other high fives. Family members pressed in to congratulate their graduates. I headed for the side door.

Outside, Tara had heard the tumult, started the van, and pulled up to the curb nearest to the auditorium. I jumped into the passenger seat she had cleared for me. In her favorite athletic top and shorts, her hair back in a braid, I thought Tara even more beautiful than she was the night of the prom.

"Congratulations, graduate," she said with her husky voice and leaned over to give me a quick smack on the lips. I directed her to the spot I'd parked the Corolla and retrieved my backpack and sleeping bag. Then she sped away as others began exiting through the main doors. "We're on our way!" she squealed. "Did you bring the money?"

Somehow the emotions of the moment made speaking difficult. "Yes, I've got the money."

"California, here we come!" she shouted and steered toward I-10 west.

Many conflicting emotions made me dizzy. Leaving Mobile? Desire for Tara? Breaking Mom and Dad's hearts? Freedom and adventure? The long haul? Seeing new places? True love?

"Wait, Tara. Please pull over. Let's talk for a minute."

Tara looked at me with concern. "You're not getting cold feet, are you?"

"No. No. I want to go. I've waited all my life to go. I just need a minute."

"All right." She slowed and pulled into a parking lot. "So, what do you want to talk about?"

I sat quietly for a minute. "Our future. What do you think it holds?"

"A hell of a lot of fun together," she answered brightly.

I couldn't help but laugh at her gift of simplicity. "What after that?"

"What, what after that? Who knows?"

"Do you want to ever complete your education?"

Another look of concern crossed her face. "Maybe . . . someday. There's plenty of time for that for both of us."

Unexpectedly the memory of the Cajun girl, Evangeline, who had spent her lifetime searching for her lost love, Gabriel, came to my mind. "Tara, I love you, you know. Do you love me?"

She looked at me with a new expression, bewilderment. "What is love?"

I didn't know how to answer at first. Then slowly I pieced some words together. "Love is a feeling that you need someone, that you always want to be with them. And love is a commitment to do what's necessary to live a lifetime together."

Tara sat for several long minutes, thinking. Then she spoke slowly. "Sorry, Jeremy. I do like you. And I really want you to go with me. We could have a lot of fun together. But I can't say I love you like that."

In an instant, all my dreams crashed, bringing me back to a place of no plans and no hope. And yet I felt a certain relief as well.

"Tara, I want to hold out for a true love. A true love like my mother and father have even if they *are* fossils."

She didn't react at first. Then she shrugged and spoke lightly. "Okay. But when you think about me, Jeremy Parker, remember that I did care enough about you to tell you the truth—even though I didn't have to."

I nodded. "Thank you for that, Tara." I grabbed my backpack, pulled out some bills from the college savings, and counted out $500. "This is to get you that new radiator." Then I counted out another $500. "And this should get you to California."

Tara took the money. "Thanks." Then she wiped away a little tear. "You're a good man, Jeremy. The best man I've ever met."

I noticed Tara had called me a man. It felt somehow noble to be called a good man. And for the first time, I felt it was true. I opened the passenger side door and stepped out with my backpack and sleeping bag.

"Don't you need me to drive you home?"

"No. I want to walk home by myself."

Tara got out of the van, came around, and kissed me on the cheek. One last wry smile said goodbye. "If you change your mind, email me." Then she returned to the driver's seat and drove away.

* * *

Walking home alone, I hummed the notes to the song "Alleluia." The tune comforted me in my distress. A car pulled alongside me. The driver's side window lowered. Officer Vance looked out from his patrol car. "You okay, son? Need a lift home?"

"No thank you, officer. I need to walk alone for a while."

The patrol car paced me as I walked. "That young woman break your heart, son?"

"My heart's broken. But I'm not sure which one of us broke it."

"It happens. Well, you call the station if you need me, ya hear?"

As the patrol car started to pull ahead, I shouted, "Officer Vance!" He stopped. "I just wanted to say, thanks for looking out for me. Giving me another chance."

"I think you'll be worth it, son," he answered before driving on.

I asked myself, *Will I be worth it? Will I use my second chance?* As I walked and pondered, I figured out the secret of Tara's allure. She truly followed the axiom "Be yourself." Regardless of what others thought, Tara knew who she wanted to be and acted on it. Could I follow her example and do the same? But who was I? Who did I want to be?

I interrupted my thoughts to listen to a mockingbird singing in the warm, early summer air. The bird knew who it was and acted on that. Doing so, the little bird brought joy to all who heard.

Tara's words came back to me. "You're a good *man,* Jeremy Parker." No longer a boy. Her statement gave me worth. More than worth . . . purpose. I would try to be a "good man" regardless of what others did or thought. I had decided to take responsibility for my own future. I had determined the core of who I wanted to be, a good man. That comforted me, too.

Next, I confronted the realities. As I walked, I remembered how fondly Mom and Dad had recited their good times at Auburn. For the first time, I regretted fooling away my high school years without working toward credentials to get me into a great school. *No time like too late,* I told myself.

* * *

The house lights were still burning at 3:30 a.m. when I walked up the driveway to our front door. Through the front window I saw Mom and Dad sitting together in silence and mutual grief. Their heads turned when I opened the front door. Dad's face lit up with the biggest smile he had ever given me. Mom closed her eyes in joy as tears streamed down her cheeks. Ruthie rushed up, wagging her entire body as usual.

"What's happened, Son?" asked Dad.

I put down my backpack and sleeping bag then petted Ruthie. "I'll tell you everything later. But you've both been right all along. Now I want to talk about my future. I'm afraid that I've just goofed off through high school. I've wasted my opportunities."

Mom spoke for both, "Are you thinking about college now?"

"Yes. I'm sorry that my grades and test scores aren't good enough to go to Auburn. I know others with better credentials who didn't get admitted. I'll try somewhere else."

Dad waved for me to sit down. Ruthie followed me onto the couch and put her head in my lap. "This might work," he started. "Start Auburn in summer term. Because fewer students are on campus in summer, Auburn lowers the entry requirements to enable more people to attend. Once you're enrolled as a student, you remain a student if you can keep up your grades. You'll need to make the grades on your own, though."

"You mean start a year from now?"

"No, I mean start next week. I have a client–a big donor to Auburn–who can get them to process your application quickly. He won't ask Admissions to accept you below their guidelines. But he can get them to expedite your paperwork."

"I'll make it there, Dad, if I can get in."

"I know you will, Son."

"There's something else I need to tell you both about."

"We already know about the boat and the Coast Guard," Mom said. "We just hope you learned something. You'll have to owe us for the fine the state of Alabama levies."

"I already owe you both a lot more than that."

Epilogue

* * *

I managed to just scrape into Auburn under their summer criteria. The science paper on parents' attitudes toward their teenagers probably made the difference. That summer I dealt with my grief over losing Tara by applying myself to my studies and even made all As. Later Mom reminded me that concentration was also Dad's way of dealing with heartache.

During the fall term after my first summer, Auburn's football team came from behind to beat Alabama in Tuscaloosa. What a celebration at Toomer's Corner! The team then went on to play in the national championship game. Dad somehow managed to buy two scalped tickets to the final. Mom gave me her ticket for Christmas and insisted that I go with Dad. He and I drove to Phoenix to join a mob of orange-wearers and help our Tigers defeat the Oregon Ducks. Auburn won their first national title since 1957 on the last play of the game. After the game, Dad didn't say much for a long time. He just enjoyed the fulfillment of a lifetime hope. Why did I ever think college couldn't be exciting?

At Auburn, I participated in the same Christian group as Mom and Dad had decades earlier. There I made a lot of wonderful friends. Mom was right again. There were some nice girls out there. Some of them thought me worth marrying. Several would have made anybody a good wife. For me, they weren't as spunky or passionate for a cause as Mom or as adventurous as Tara. I kept looking for my true love.

I continued improving at volleyball and played on the six-man intramural team that won the campus championship. With a teammate, I made the quarter finals of an amateur two-man beach volleyball tournament in Panama City. Mom and Dad came from Mobile to see both competitions. You'd have thought they were attending a football game. I could hear Mom's voice cheering over all the clamor.

College *was* fun and a most worthy adventure. To my own surprise, I found myself majoring in accounting to eventually support a family and help people realize their dreams like Dad did for the Hobbses. Having the goal to do well, even the coursework became interesting to me. I graduated from Auburn with honor. Like Dad had said, "What makes life meaningful is trying to do the hard things." Both Mom and Dad shed a few tears at my college graduation, so different from my high school conclusion.

My third summer as a student, I interned at a big Atlanta accounting firm. They later hired me as a temp to fill out individual income tax returns during the two following winter/spring terms. My work caught the attention of their international division. They promised me a full-time job and posting to Sydney, Australia, if I passed the CPA exam. I did pass and took the job. In Australia, I met the love of my life, Denyse, playing on a church volleyball team. A beautiful girl with Mom's spunk and passion and with an adventurous spirit like Tara's. Plus she even had a charming Aussie accent.

Oh, yes. Whatever happened to Tara, the best prom date anyone ever had? I emailed her the pictures Dad took before the prom. She returned a selfie in California by the Golden Gate Bridge. While at Auburn, I occasionally got emails from her with snapshots of her visiting various interesting places. Tara was decent enough not to tell me who took the pictures or about men she might be traveling with. Some of the emails described difficult circumstances and asked for a little money. I always responded with $100 to her PayPal account. I received one false message from someone impersonating Tara. The email claimed she had developed a heroin addiction and needed help. I was relieved to find out that it wasn't true.

Tara sent congratulations for my college graduation and again when I wrote telling her I had met and proposed to Denyse. After that I didn't hear any more from or about Tara until . . . Oops, that's another adventure for another time.

Well that's my, Jeremy Parker's, story. I made a lot of mistakes along the way as I tried to find out who I was. But I wouldn't trade any of those experiences—both good and bad—because they finally led me to the man I became. . . and to the life and love I never knew I always wanted.

Authors' Note

* * *

All the characters depicted in *Jeremy's Challenge* are purely fictional and from the imagination of the authors. Locations and settings in the Mobile area are as accurate as space and most readers' attentions will allow. Science, nature, and history backgrounds are correct according to first-hand observation and reasonable research.

Even before we published this novel, reviewers and editors expressed interest in Tara's future. At Kit's suggestion, Tara has already been incorporated as a major character into the next Dave and Katie adventure, *Challenge in the Golden State*. Jeremy will meet Tara again, as well as Giselle.

Jeremy's story incorporates some references to the University of Alabama and Auburn University–two fine schools sharing a state in a less-than-friendly rivalry. The references wholly fit Alabama's state culture, the setting for the story. I attended Auburn and after four years of hard work graduated with high honor. We needed a university as part of this story. Why not my alma mater?

At graduation, I thought the world revolved around Auburn. Indeed, my world had for four years. After graduation, I learned that nearly everyone feels the same about their school. Auburn is a good school–not exceptional according to national rating services comparing colleges and universities. The logical and honest side of me has pondered, *Why do you have such lifetime loyalty for a place that knew you only as student 7075210 and not at all after graduating?*

Auburn did give me an education that led to a wonderful career. That's not enough to explain my loyalty. Rather, I've come to realize that my feelings are based not on the school itself, but on my experiences there. Many "never before/always after" experiences were compressed into four adventurous years. I started Auburn at seventeen (and immature even for that age), and like Dave said in the story, I was like an outline of a person in a coloring book. I left Auburn colored in. At Auburn, I made decisions about who I would be for a lifetime. Auburn provided the nest in which adult Drew hatched.

One other factor explains my feelings of joy associated with Auburn. I've not remained in touch with many of my Auburn friends. But I pray for them sometimes, wherever they might be. Whenever Auburn manages a major sports victory or news highlight, I'm happy for those friends and share a disconnected moment of joy with them. Memories can be like mining joy from the past for your current life. My prayer for you is to embrace eras of your life that give you joy to recall.

Love ya always, Auburn,

Drew Coons

What is a more than ordinary life?

Each person's life is unique and special. In that sense, there is no such thing as an ordinary life. However, many people yearn for lives more special: excitement, adventure, romance, purpose, character. Our site is dedicated to the premise that any life can be more than ordinary.

At **MoreThanOrdinaryLives.com** you will find:

- inspiring stories
- entertaining novels
- ideas and resources
- free downloads

https://morethanordinarylives.com/

Novels by Kit and Drew Coons

"Challenge for Two has characters that are more than colorful!! The settings from the downtown diner to the mansion are charming. It gave me so much pure reading pleasure. Looking forward to the next adventure with Dave and Katie." **Marnie Rasche**

A series of difficult circumstances has forced Dave and Katie Parker into early retirement. Searching for new life and purpose, the Parkers take a wintertime job house sitting an old Victorian mansion. The picturesque river town in southeastern Minnesota is far from the climate and culture of their home near the Alabama Gulf Coast.

But dark secrets sleep in the mansion. A criminal network has ruthlessly intimidated the community since the timber baron era of the 19th century. Residents have been conditioned to look the other way.

The Parkers' questions about local history and clues they discover in the mansion bring an evil past to light and create division in the small community. While some fear the consequences of digging up the truth, others want freedom from crime and justice for victims. Faced with personal threats, the Parkers must decide how to respond for themselves and for the good of the community.

"Challenge Down Under is a gripping story of the rawness of life when desperation hits and of the power of love in the most difficult circumstances. I couldn't put this book down. I'm a born and bred New Zealander, and I love how the Coonses captured the heart of both city and country life Down Under. You will fall in love with the colorful characters and be intrigued by where curiosity and love can take a person." **Jill Rangeley of Auckland, NZ**

Dave and Katie Parker's only son, Jeremy, is getting married in Australia. Despite initial reservations, the Parkers discover that Denyse is perfect for Jeremy and that she's the daughter they've always wanted. But she brings with her a colorful and largely dysfunctional Aussie family. Again Dave and Katie are fish out of water as they try to relate to a boisterous clan in a culture very different from their home in south Alabama.

After the wedding, Denyse feels heartbroken that her younger brother, Trevor, did not attend. Details emerge that lead Denyse to believe her brother may be in trouble. Impressed by his parents' sleuthing experience in Minnesota, Jeremy volunteers them to locate Trevor. Their search leads them on an adventure through Australia and New Zealand.

Others are also searching for Trevor, with far more sinister intentions. With a talent for irresponsible chicanery inherited from his family, Trevor has left a trail of trouble in his wake.

"Adventure finds Dave and Katie even at home. Mobile and the Gulf Coast are the sultry setting for the couples' latest foray into a world of corruption, extortion, and racial tension. Thick southern charm and potential financial ruin swirl about them as they strive to serve those they love. A fast-paced and engaging story with colorful characters. A great read!" Leslie Mercer

Dave and Katie Parker regret that their only child Jeremy, his Australian wife Denyse, and their infant daughter live on the opposite side of the world. Unexpectedly, Jeremy calls to ask his father's help finding an accounting job in the US. The Parkers risk their financial security by purchasing full ownership of the struggling firm to make a place for Jeremy.

Denyse finds south Alabama fascinating compared to her native Australia. She quickly resumes her passion for teaching inner-city teenagers. Invited by Katie, other colorful guests arrive from Australia and Minnesota to experience gulf coast culture. Aided by their guests, Dave and Katie examine their faith after Katie receives discouraging news from her doctors.

Political, financial, and racial tensions have been building in Mobile. Dave and Katie are pulled into a crisis that requires them to rise to a new level of more than ordinary.

"The Ambassadors combines elements of science fiction and real-life genetics into a story that is smart, witty, and completely unique. Drew and Kit Coons navigate complex issues of humanity in a way that will leave you pondering the implications long after the book is over. If you're ready for a compelling adventure with humor, suspense, and protagonists you can really root for, don't miss out on this one!" **Jayna Richardson**

Two genetically engineered beings unexpectedly arrive on Earth. Unlike most extraterrestrials depicted in science fiction, the pair is attractive, personable, and telegenic--the perfect talk-show guests. They have come to Earth as ambassadors bringing an offer of partnership in a confederation of civilizations. Technological advances are offered as part of the partnership. But humans must learn to cooperate among themselves to join.

Molly, a young reporter, and Paul, a NASA scientist, have each suffered personal tragedy and carry emotional baggage. They are asked to tutor the ambassadors in human ways and to guide them on a worldwide goodwill tour. Molly and Paul observe as the extraterrestrials commit faux pas while experiencing human culture. They struggle trying to define a romance and partnership while dealing with burdens of the past.

However, mankind finds implementing actual change difficult. Clashing value systems and conflicts among subgroups of humanity erupt. Inevitably, rather than face difficult choices, fearmongers in the media start to blame the messengers. Then an uncontrolled biological weapon previously created by a rogue country tips the world into chaos. Molly, Paul, and the others must face complex moral decisions about what being human means and the future of mankind.

Life-skills Books

More Than Ordinary *Challenges*—Dealing with the Unexpected (Group Discussion Questions Included)

Many heartwarming stories share about difficult situations that worked out miraculously or through iron-willed determination. The stories are useful in that they inspire hope. But sometimes life just doesn't work out the way we expected. Many people's lives will never be what they had hoped. What does a person do then? This life-skills book uses our personal struggle with infertility as an example.

More Than Ordinary *Choices*—Making Good Decisions (Group Discussion Questions Included)

Every moment separates our lives into before and after. Some moments divide our lives into never before and always after. Many of those life-changing moments are based on the choices we make. God allows us to make choices through free will. Making good choices at those moments is for our good and ultimately reflects on God as we represent Him in this world.

More Than Ordinary *Marriage*—A Higher Level

Some might suggest that any marriage surviving in these times is more than ordinary. Unfortunately, many marriages don't last a lifetime. But by more than ordinary, we mean a marriage that goes beyond basic survival and is more than successful. This type of relationship can cause others to ask, "What makes their marriage so special?" Such marriages glorify God and represent Christ and the church well.

More Than Ordinary *Faith*—Why Does God Allow Suffering? (Group Discussion Questions Included)

Why does God allow suffering? This is a universal question in every heart. The question is both reasonable and valid. Lack of a meaningful answer is a faith barrier for many. Shallow answers can undermine faith. Fortunately, the Bible gives clear reasons that God allows suffering. But the best time to learn about God's purposes and strengthen our faith is *before* a crisis.

More Than Ordinary *Wisdom*—Stories of Faith and Folly

Jesus told story after story to communicate God's truth. Personal stories create hope and change lives by speaking to the heart. The following collection of Drew's stories is offered for your amusement and so that you can learn from his experiences. We hope these stories will motivate you to consider your own life experiences. What was God teaching you? "Let the redeemed of the Lord tell their story." (Psalm 107:2)

More Than Ordinary *Abundance*—From Kit's Heart

Abundance means, "richly or plentifully supplied; ample." Kit's personal devotions in this mini book record her experiences of God's abundant goodness and offer insights into godly living. Her hope is that you will rejoice with her and marvel at God's provision in your own life. "They celebrate your abundant goodness and joyfully sing of your righteousness." (Psalm 145:7)

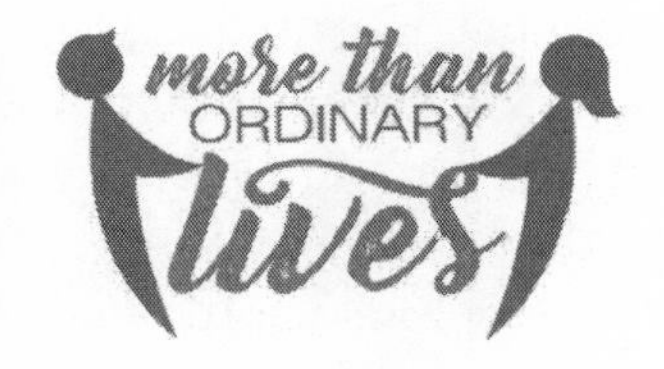

https://morethanordinarylives.com

New for 2020

Challenge in the Golden State

The Parker family travels in an RV to the Golden State on vacation. After Dave, Katie, Jeremy, Denyse, and Katelyn enjoy Southern California's glamorous attractions, the family separates at LA's airport. Denyse takes her daughter, Katelyn, to visit her family in Australia. Jeremy returns to Mobile to manage the Parkers' accounting firm. Dave and Katie meander north to experience more of California's wonders.

At a state park, Katie discovers two bodies—the victims of a prescription opioid overdose. A man is already dead. The other—a teenaged girl—barely survives. The small town of Redwood Hills is situated among giant trees between California's rugged coastline and picturesque wine country. The community has suffered an escalating rash of tragic overdoses. Sympathy for the girl draws Dave and Katie into an investigation to discover the source of illicit drugs.

Criminal elements of the community are threatened as Dave and Katie find evidence of a wicked scheme. Dave is poisoned by an unknown opponent. Planted false evidence results in Dave and Katie being arrested, indicted, and court-ordered to remain local. They have no one to trust and summon Jeremy and Denyse for assistance. But their son and daughter-in-law are each facing their own crises. Both need help from Dave and Katie. An unexpected source comes to Dave and Katie's aid as they pursue the truth and exoneration.

Made in the USA
Monee, IL
24 November 2021